"We'd better hit the water before one of those older gentlemen has a heart attack!"

Tom murmured, catching her hand to drag her along the sand.

"Oh? Is this swimsuit too bold?" Paula waded thigh-deep into the cool water.

"Well, let me see." He confronted her sternly, running his palms up the sides of her bare legs. "Nothing objectionable there."

Before she realized what he was doing, his hands cupped her breasts, and the thumbs stroked the sensitive inner edges bared by the low neckline. "No one could object to that," he concluded, brushing her nipples lightly through the stretch fabric before pulling her deeper into the water.

"What do you think you're doing?" Her protests were drowned in the wave that broke over them, and she spluttered furiously.

Tom smiled. "Just checking you over..."

To Have and to Hold books by
Jacqueline Topaz

DEEPER THAN DESIRE #39

Jacqueline Topaz, *a news reporter for the Associated Press, covers theater, art, and dance in Southern California. After graduating from Brandeis University, she lived in Italy for a year on a playwriting fellowship. Among Jackie's loves: participating in her writers' group, going to the theater, and growing roses. She and her husband live in La Habra, California.*

Dear Reader:

February is a good month for romance — not only because Valentine's Day falls on the fourteenth, but also because in so much of the country, freezing temperatures and snowy blasts make you want to snuggle up with someone you love. And when you're not curling close, you can read SECOND CHANCE AT LOVE romances! They, too, are guaranteed to keep you toasty warm and wonderfully satisfied.

We begin the month with *Notorious* (#244) by Karen Keast. Many of you wrote in to compliment Karen on the superb job she did on her first book, *Suddenly the Magic* (#255, October 1984). In *Notorious* she's written a boldly sensual variation on *The Taming of the Shrew*, except in this case veterinarian Kate Hollister sets out to domesticate decadent playboy photographer Drew Cambridge — once she realizes she can't resist him, that is! You'll love watching Kate transform this devil-may-care womanizer into a perfect lover . . . and husband!

Have you ever wondered how magicians bend keys and saw people in half? These intriguing secrets — and more! — are revealed in Lee Williams's most original, riveting romance yet — *Under His Spell* (#245). A phony psychic, a sleek, slobbering leopard, and sexy, black-garbed magician Julian Sharpe make *Under His Spell* an unforgettable romance with a *very* magic touch.

We were pleased and impressed with Carole Buck's first romance for us, *Encore* (#219, September 1984). Now *Intruder's Kiss* (#246) establishes her as one of our brightest talents. I love the opening: Sara Edwards, armed with a squash racquet, is about to tackle two noisy intruders — who turn out to be a huge sheep dog and charming, devastating Matt Michaels. Although wildly attracted to Matt (not the dog!), Sara begins to wonder: Just who *is* Matt Michaels? You'll be delightfully entertained by this lively, sexy, fun-filled tale.

Few writers capture the sizzling chemistry between a hero and heroine better than Elissa Curry. In *Lady Be Good*

(#247), she creates two truly unique characters: Etiquette columnist Grace Barrett is poised and polished, perfectly coiffed and regally mannered; Luke "the Laser" Lazurnovich is an ex-football player who pretends to be even more uncouth than he really is. To tell how this ill-matched pair comes to realize they're perfect for each other, Elissa combines a delicious sense of humor with the endearing tenderness of an emotionally involving love story.

In her outstanding debut, *Sparring Partners* (#177, February 1984), Lauren Fox immediately established herself as a master of witty dialogue. Now, very much in the Lauren Fox tradition, comes *A Clash of Wills* (#248), which pits calm, controlled stockbroker Carrie Carstairs against outrageous, impulsive, infuriatingly stubborn investor/inventor Harlen Matthews. As you can imagine, they're an explosive combination. *A Clash of Wills* is wonderfully fresh and inventive.

You'll be *Swept Away* by our last February SECOND CHANCE AT LOVE romance, #249 by Jacqueline Topaz. "Cleaning woman" Paula Ward has dusted Tom Clinton's penthouse and is "borrowing" his lavish bathroom to prepare for a date, when the devastating millionaire arrives home — with guests! To save her job, Paula impulsively agrees to pose as Tom's wife — with funny, sad, and, above all, sensuous results . . .

February's SECOND CHANCE AT LOVE romances are sure to chase away your winter blahs. So enjoy them — and keep warm!

With best wishes,

Ellen Edwards

Ellen Edwards, Senior Editor
SECOND CHANCE AT LOVE
The Berkley Publishing Group
200 Madison Avenue
New York, N.Y. 10016

SWEPT AWAY

JACQUELINE TOPAZ

A SECOND CHANCE AT LOVE BOOK

SWEPT AWAY

First edition published February 1985

First printing

Printed in the United States of America

Second Chance at Love books are published by
The Berkley Publishing Group
200 Madison Avenue, New York, NY 10016

For Kathe Brockman

SWEPT AWAY

CHAPTER
One

PAULA WARD SCOOTED the industrial vacuum cleaner into the hall and turned to give the penthouse apartment a final survey.

Not a speck of dirt in sight—and whoever designed this apartment certainly didn't have the cleaning lady in mind, she reflected, running one hand through her shaggy blond hair.

Cream, cream, everywhere—cream couch, ivory carpet, off-white drapes—plus lots of light oak furniture that had to be carefully oiled. All the tabletops were glass, and she'd spent half an hour wiping down the three computers in the study.

The Picasso was crooked, Paula decided, and stepped into the room, closing the door behind her. She adjusted the etching and regarded the nude figure hopefully, as if the mere presence of great art might sweep away her weariness.

No such luck.

It was five-thirty, according to a discreet wall clock with modernistic hands that almost defied interpretation. Or maybe it was six twenty-five. Anyway, it was Friday.

Got to get my watch out of hock, Paula thought ruefully. It was sitting at the jeweler's, newly fixed, and she couldn't scrape up the fifteen dollars to redeem it until . . . when?

Never mind. The day and the week were over, and that fact accomplished what the artwork hadn't.

Her energy rebounding in a little thrill of excitement, Paula ducked into the bedroom, flipping on the cassette player-radio as she walked through.

Her expression brightened at the sight of her hot-pink dress on the inside of the bathroom door. On the counter, her purse sat open, revealing a cache of cosmetics.

This was no ordinary bathroom, of course. It looked like something out of the *Arabian Nights:* a vast expanse of tile, a sunken tub, mirrors along one wall, double sinks, everything decorated in light gray and maroon. Spotless, too. She ought to know; she'd cleaned it.

Now if I were Sally, Paula mused as she slipped out of her white uniform to reveal a pink lace slip, I'd be changing in one of those industrial-looking rest rooms downstairs.

She smiled at the thought of her roommate. They were opposites: Sally, wary and suspicious of life; Paula, impulsive and freewheeling. They had two things in common, though: husbands who'd left them almost penniless and the cleaning business they'd started as a way to make ends meet.

Humming, Paula splashed water over her face. The party at the restaurant down the street probably wouldn't be anything much. She'd have a drink at the hosted bar, talk nonsense with men whose hastily removed wedding rings left white ghosts, and go home with Sally.

This was the delicious part: changing her clothes in Thomas C. Clinton III's apartment high atop the Clinton Computers Building.

Paula applied rose-scented lotion to her face and hands. She almost wished she could stay here in the luxury of this penthouse, with the soft purr of the radio to keep her company and the air-conditioner to protect her from the heat of a Southern California July.

But the mysterious Thomas C. Clinton III himself would be coming back from New York tomorrow. Paula pictured a paunchy, balding businessman and giggled, wondering what he'd think if he saw her here.

Perhaps he was married—Thomas C. Clinton was notoriously secretive about his private life—but she doubted it. This apartment, sitting in isolated splendor above a twelve-story office building, lacked a woman's touch.

She wrinkled her nose at herself in the mirror as she began applying mascara the same shade of blue as her eyes. No doubt Thomas Clinton's moneybags kept him warm at night.

If so, he must be feeling a distinct chill, she decided, her thoughts flying back to the business section she'd spotted in the study. She couldn't help noticing the article about Clinton Computers' financial woes.

She'd looked for a photograph of the great man himself, but the only one she found, a framed family grouping on the wall, had obviously been taken many years ago. It showed two stern-looking adults, a young girl in a wheelchair, and a reedy boy standing behind his sister. She wasn't even sure if Clinton was the father or the son.

In any case, Paula could certainly sympathize with financial problems. The cleaning business had been dragging along until this past week, when they snared a one-month trial contract to clean the top three floors of the Clinton Building.

Foundation. Blusher. Mascara. Lipstick. A dab of perfume. She felt like a new woman—or a rebuilt one, anyway.

Paula whirled in front of the bank of mirrors like a star in an old-time Hollywood movie, gyrating to an upbeat song and noting how the pink lace flattered the tan on her long slender legs. The slip was costly, left over from a shopping spree Mickey had encouraged her to take, before he lost everything.

Now what to do about this mop of hair? Paula regarded her thick blond mane in the mirror. Sally had studied to be a beautician before she got married, but that was way back when shag haircuts were in style. And that was what she'd given Paula.

Great. I look like Lassie.

Piled up on top of her head with one hand, the hair looked halfway decent. Too bad she couldn't walk around with one hand stuck on top of her head to keep it that way.

"Oh, I'm so lonesome, and I'm feelin' so blue," she sang along with the radio, and wiggled her hips again.

Then came the sound that froze Paula's blood: the sound of the bedroom door closing, followed by the radio clicking off.

Oh, Lord, there's somebody else in here.

Her heart had relocated to somewhere in her throat. It thumped there crazily as, ever so slowly, Paula pushed open the bathroom door.

By the time she realized what a stupid move she'd made, it was too late. She'd been seen.

"What on earth?" The man who stood by the bed

didn't look like a mugger, she noted with a glimmer of hope. Three-piece suit, dark blue, possibly silk. Light-brown hair so exquisitely cut it looked as if it grew that way. He was tall and well-built, with tan eyes that could be described only as seriously annoyed.

"Hi," she said.

"What the hell are you doing in my apartment?"

That answered the question of who he was. "You weren't supposed to be back till tomorrow."

"Someone in this room isn't making sense, and I don't think it's me." His jaw worked angrily, but he stayed where he was.

Paula had the uncomfortable feeling those eyes were taking in every exposed inch of her above and below the wispy slip. "I. . . . I was just changing. Oh, please don't fire me, Mr. Clinton!"

"How can I fire you when I don't even know who you are?"

"I'm the cleaning lady. Your manager hired me last week." She gazed up at him with pleading eyes and was relieved to see a glint of humor in that steely expression.

"Well, your timing is lousy," he said more mildly. "I'm going to have to do some fast explaining."

"Why? . . ."

Someone outside turned the doorknob, and a man's voice called, "Tom? Is everything okay?"

"Don't come in!" Paula cried without thinking. "I'm not dressed."

The door was pulled quickly shut.

"Why in heaven's name did you do that?" Her employer sank down on the bed with a groan. "This is all I needed. This is just great."

"I'm sorry." Torn between wanting to comfort him and wanting to put her clothes on, Paula fluttered in the doorway. "Sometimes I blurt things out without thinking. I'll just put on my uniform and go tell your friend who I am."

"No!" The man caught her wrist as she started past him and pulled her down beside him on the bed. For a crazy moment Paula wondered if he was going to kiss her and wasn't at all sure she'd mind.

"Listen closely." As he spoke, she could almost see the gears turning in his head. "The people out there are Mr. and Mrs. Jensen. Arthur and Louise. Can you remember that?"

"Arthur and Louise Jensen," she repeated. "Okay."

"They are very, very important people. Never mind why. I haven't got time to explain. The thing you need to know is that they are also very, very strait-laced. The mere thought of my having an unclad woman in my apartment is enough to scotch the most important deal of my life. Have you got that?"

Paula gulped. "Yes. Do you want me to climb out the window?"

His shoulders shook with surprised, silent laughter. "Are you some kind of human fly?"

"Oh. I forgot where I was."

The man took her hands in his and examined them. At first Paula thought he was looking for telltale cleaning-lady roughness, but instead he tapped the small opal ring she wore on her right hand. It had been a present from her father when she graduated from high school.

"Put it on your left hand," he said. "Now go in there and get dressed. When you come out, you are going to be Mrs. Clinton. What's your first name?"

"Paula." She gaped up at him for a moment, not sure that he really meant to go through with this.

"Well? Hurry up," he said.

She stood, indecisive. But what else could she do? "Thanks, Mr. Clinton. I promise I'll never do anything like this again."

"You call your husband by his first name," he said. "It happens to be Tom."

"Tom." She scurried into the bathroom and closed the door behind her.

She'd really done it this time, Paula thought as she slipped on the hot-pink dress and wadded up her uniform, looking for a place to stash it. Under the sink.

Oh, honestly, she scolded herself when she realized what she'd done. Do you think Mrs. Jensen is going to go through his closets and notice a cleaning woman's uniform? Well, the thing needed laundering anyway.

Nothing to be done about the hair except a quick brushing. Ring transferred to the left hand. Ready. Ready to play the wife of a millionaire she'd never met before to a couple who could be anybody. Anybody very, very important.

At least the place was clean.

Paula slipped on her high heels and walked into the living room.

Against the far wall, Tom was fixing drinks at the bar. In between, an older couple sat on the couch with their backs to Paula, the woman's graying hair styled short and classic à la Nancy Reagan.

"Hello, everybody," Paula called with what she hoped was a touch of gaiety. "Please excuse my tardiness. I lost track of the time."

Tom made the introductions. Mr. Jensen rose politely, but Paula waved him back to his seat.

Now what? Was she supposed to fix hors d'oeuvres? Should she ask them how they liked Anaheim, or did they live in the area?

"Isn't this heat terrible?" Paula sat in an armchair facing them.

"Yes. We're not used to it, living in San Francisco," said Mrs. Jensen.

So much for that subject.

Mr. Jensen was eyeing something on the wall behind her. The Picasso. The Picasso etching of a nude woman.

"Oh, I hope you're not offended," Paula blithered. "The picture is a bit risqué for Tom and me, but it was a gift from my aunt and, well, we couldn't hurt her feelings."

Mr. Jensen nodded understandingly. Whew!

Tom handed their guests glasses of orange juice and provided Paula with the same. She could have used a drink.

"Where are we going for dinner?" asked Mr. Jensen.

Dinner? Paula gulped. That meant a whole evening together.

Tom suggested several restaurants. The Jensens settled on steak and seafood.

"I hope you don't mind if we eat now," Mrs. Jensen said. "We're used to dining rather early."

"Oh, that's fine with me. I'm starved." Paula fixed the couple with her brightest smile and glanced at the modernistic clock. She still couldn't tell what time it was.

The next few hours remained forever a blur in her memory. They rode in Tom's Cadillac to a restaurant with a nautical name where they chattered inanely about sports and other safe topics.

Paula considered ordering the least expensive thing on the menu— chicken—but decided Tom wouldn't notice anyway. The lobster was delicious.

From time to time she sneaked sidelong glances at her boss. He wasn't so much handsome, she concluded, as riveting—intense, aware, taking in all available data at every moment and sorting it as thoroughly as a computer. She knew that look. She'd seen it on Mickey's face when he was gambling.

Mr. and Mrs. Jensen declined to come in when they returned to the Clinton Building. Their chauffeur had been called for nine o'clock, and indeed, there he was, sitting in a Rolls-Royce by the curb.

Paula had never in her life known such relief as when she bade the couple good-bye. Until...

"I know this is awfully short notice, but we didn't realize Tom was married," Mrs. Jensen told Paula. "We're staying with one of our partners in Malibu, and he's having a party at his beach house this weekend. We'd love for you to come."

"He wanted to invite you, Tom, but he didn't think you'd feel comfortable with the rest of us couples," added her husband. "But under the circumstances, I know he'd want us to extend the invitation. Come down Saturday morning and stay over."

"We'd be delighted," said Tom.

Paula choked, and Mr. Jensen had to pound her on the back. "I...I...I'm afraid my parents' anniversary party is Saturday night." They couldn't possibly know her parents lived in Delaware.

Tom was glaring at her. Paula shot him a helpless look. She wondered irrelevantly what the chauffeur, standing starchily by the open car door, thought of this scene.

"I've got an idea," said Mrs. Jensen. "Why don't the two of you come for lunch on Saturday? Bring your bathing suits and enjoy the beach. You can get back in plenty of time."

Much as Paula dreaded the prospect, she had a feeling her job was at stake. And she and Sally needed this account. "What a wonderful idea."

The couple provided the time and location. It seemed like forever before the taillights of the Rolls-Royce disappeared down the street.

"Upstairs," Tom said tersely. Paula's thoughts of fleeing into the night withered and died.

They entered the building through a side door and traveled up in the elevator. It was an eerie feeling, being all alone in this building at night. Twelve stories of empty offices, with maybe a night watchman somewhere in the maze. And the two of them.

At least the apartment looked normal enough, and Paula's spirits perked up at the familiar surroundings.

"You deserve a drink." Tom poured two glasses of sherry and carried them over to the couch. He sat beside her.

"About tomorrow," she began. "Couldn't you go by yourself?"

"You were a big hit." Propping his feet up on the coffee table—no wonder the glass had been such a mess—he regarded her cheerfully. "I'd never have been invited by myself. Why didn't I think of getting married sooner?"

"You mean you'd get married just to pull off a deal?" This man had a reputation as a successful entrepreneur, but Paula had never known anyone to carry business that far.

"At this point, I'd do just about anything," Tom admitted. "There's a lot riding on this—You'd better start on that drink, Paula. This is a long story."

Clinton Computers, he explained, had been hit hard by the home-computer glut.

"We lost money last year," he said. "A lot of it." He had to expand or die. So Tom Clinton had sat down with his best engineers and worked out the plans for a high-capacity small computer with a built-in device to make it software-compatible with any other computer.

"It's a natural," said Tom. "A revolution. Right this minute. Two years from now, everybody will have one."

He needed major funding right away. Due to the company's bleak performance the previous year, conventional lending institutions were out. That left venture capital—private investors willing to take a calculated risk in return for the possibility of making a lot of money.

"The Jensens have a partnership with two other couples," he said. "All conservative, although not quite so much as the Jensens."

Paula sighed and put her feet up on the coffee table beside his. No harder to clean up two sets of scuff marks than one.

"I suppose I let myself in for this," she admitted. "Honestly, Tom, what did you expect me to do when you accepted for the weekend? Share a room with you?"

"I wasn't thinking about that. But now that you mention it..."

In a blink, his eyes cleared of the shrewd, speculative look that had accompanied his business musings, and he saw her as a woman. Paula could read his response in the sudden intake of breath and the way his tan eyes traveled down her body, past the soft swell of breasts to the nipped-in waist and long legs.

"Maybe that wouldn't be such a bad idea," he murmured.

"Hey!" She sat up indignantly. "Just because I work for you doesn't mean you should go getting ideas."

She caught a glimpse of a devilish grin as Tom moved toward her. "We're married, remember?" His mouth closed over hers, tasting sweet and full of desire.

Oh, no. Paula hadn't been held in a man's arms since the divorce a year ago, and to her dismay she found herself kissing him back hungrily. What were her hands doing twined around his neck? Why was she leaning toward him as if she wanted to be held tight?

For some reason Tom seemed to have gotten the idea she was enjoying this.

Maybe it was the fact that she was heatedly kissing that smile off his lips. Or the way her fingers feathered along his back, reaching beneath jacket and shirt to touch the bare skin. Or the way she gasped softly when he nipped at her earlobe and traced her jawline with his tongue.

"What are you doing?" She forced herself back and stared at him perplexed.

"Teaching you how to be a good wife. We aren't finished." His finger traced the deep neckline of her dress.

"Oh, yes, we are." Paula stood up and strode through the apartment to collect her rumpled uniform. "I've been married before. I know all the rules and all the ways they get broken."

"Sounds like you had a pretty rotten experience."

Tom stood in the bedroom doorway, half blocking her exit.

"There's nothing more boring than someone who complains about their ex-spouse," said Paula. "Let's just say I gambled on him and he gambled on anything that moved."

She thought for one naive moment that she could just step over Tom's leg and get through the door. Instead, he shifted himself and cornered her against the frame.

"What are you doing?"

"Unfinished business." His hands cupped her face as his tongue penetrated her mouth.

There was no buffer of air between them as they stood stretched against each other. Paula tried to push him back, but his weight pinned her.

The problem was that his hard body felt so incredibly good against her softness. Paula hadn't realized how thirsty her skin had grown, how her palms would drink in the rough texture of his neck and the smoothness of his back. His back. She was doing it again, reaching up there beneath the clothes to stroke him.

"Stop!" She struggled against him, and he paused.

"Am I hurting you?"

"No. Yes. Let me go!" She hurtled away into the living room. "I have to leave."

"Meet me in front of the building tomorrow morning. Eight-thirty." He looked as if he wanted to say something else, something personal, but the words that came out were, "Bring your bathing suit. You'll be smashing."

"Okay. But no more parties! No more masquerades! Tomorrow clears the debt, right?" She backed away across the carpet and turned to flee.

"Paula!"

"What?"

"You dropped your uniform." He laughed as he tossed it to her. "Feel free to change clothes here any time."

Her face burning with embarrassment, Paula hurried into the hall. She barely caught herself in time to avoid tripping over the industrial vacuum cleaner.

Resignedly, she wheeled it down the hall to the closet. One more day in the life of a cleaning lady.

All the way home she wondered what it would be like to eat lobster every night and live atop a twelve-story building and go to bed with Tom Clinton.

CHAPTER
Two

WHEN PAULA DROVE up the next day in her battered Chevy, Tom was leaning against a Porsche by the curb. Evidently the Cadillac wouldn't do for casual use.

Not that Tom looked all that casual himself. Clad in gray slacks and a navy polo shirt, he appeared crisp and fresh despite the ninety-degree heat.

"Hi." She retrieved her beach bag and slid out of the car. Her thighs, exposed by the white short shorts, clung painfully to the seat. "Ouch!"

Tom let out a low wolf whistle.

"Am I underdressed?" Paula glanced nervously down at her trim halter top, shorts, and high-heeled sandals.

"Not for a beach party." Tom slipped one arm around her bare waist and took the bag. "The men will enjoy ogling you, and the women won't mind because you're safely married to me."

"What if I make a slip?" she asked as he tucked

her into the sports car. "Suppose I say something about my work or my roommate?"

Tom started the engine and turned up the air conditioning. "You and your former roommate are still close friends, and you refer to her by that term. As for work—you mean volunteer work. Charity."

Paula leaned against the door as they sped down the street toward the freeway. "Speaking of my roommate, Sally thinks this whole thing is crazy."

That was putting it mildly. Sally had been furious when she learned how Paula had jeopardized their new contract.

"Of course it's crazy," Tom said jauntily. "You have to learn to judge things by their outcome, Paula."

"You sound like my ex-husband when he lost money at the track," she muttered.

"I don't bet on horses." Tom steered up the freeway on-ramp. "The odds are lousy."

"What if you don't get the loan?"

His expression tightened. "I'll get the money . . . somehow."

"You make it sound desperate," Paula said. "Is the Mafia after you or something?"

That startled a chuckle out of him. "No, I . . . I have plans. If I hadn't been so wrapped up in myself before . . . well, let's just say I woke up a little late. But I don't give in easily."

Plans. Were they like Mickey's plans, always some wild scheme, just out of reach?

I don't need to go through that again, she reflected. I need a husband who's steady enough to raise a family.

She looked over at Tom's profile, at the mischievous tilt to his mouth and the speculative gleam in his eye as he contemplated the adventure ahead.

Paula's heart indulged in a brief breakdance spin. Okay, okay, so she wanted someone solid and dependable. But not yet.

"I guess dealing with the Jensens is having a greater effect on me than I'd thought." Tom frowned. "My neck and shoulders are tied up in knots. How about a back rub?"

"Sure." It was a long drive, over an hour, and Paula could appreciate his discomfort. Besides, she was good at giving back rubs.

She knelt on the seat and caught his shoulder muscles between her thumb and fingers. Firmly, she kneaded them, finding the knots of tension and working them loose.

Why was it that the back of a man's neck looked so vulnerable? she wondered as she massaged. His hair brushed across her hand, teasingly intimate.

"That feels fantastic." Tom half closed his eyes, but kept his attention on the freeway. "Don't stop."

Paula reached to rub the muscles on his far side. Her breasts brushed against his arm, and to her embarrassment, the peaks tightened instinctively.

Surely he hadn't noticed. She resumed her ministrations to his back, feeling him relax at her touch.

"Are you okay?" she asked at last. "My fingers are getting tired."

"That's fine. Listen, you can massage me any time."

Paula laughed. "Sally and I missed our calling. We could have made a lot more money as masseuses."

"Yes, and gotten into a lot more trouble, too," he pointed out.

She settled back on the seat, watching the Los Angeles skyline slip past. "Hey, does it look awfully smoggy to you?"

"Now that you mention it, yes. There's a smog alert out for today."

As they approached Santa Monica and the highway that would take them to Malibu, the sky inland turned a deep brown and Paula could smell smoke.

"That's not smog, it's a brush fire," she said.

Tom flicked on the radio and found an all-news station. They had to listen to three commercials and a Washington roundup before the announcer told them what they wanted to know. Two major fires were burning out of control in the Santa Monica Mountains and Topanga Canyon.

"Maybe we should turn back," Paula said. "Didn't one of those burn all the way to the sea a few years ago?"

"Getting cold feet?" Tom said. "You know as well as I do the fire isn't anywhere near Malibu."

"I suppose you're right." Brush fires were a fact of life in Southern California, roaring through the wilderness and sometimes veering into populated regions when weather conditions were right.

And they were certainly right at the moment, the announcer said: high temperatures, extremely low humidity, and in canyon areas, winds gusting up to ninety miles per hour.

But Paula didn't let this faze her. Under ordinary circumstances, she and Sally would have spent the day cramming their bodies onto the beach at Newport amid gangly teenagers and overweight matrons. Instead, she was getting a chance to see one of the fabulous beach houses at Malibu, the area famed for its hot and cold running movie stars.

The Porsche passed through the town of Malibu. Paula peered up the drive toward the J. Paul Getty Museum, but couldn't see it through the trees. She'd visited once, impressed less by the artworks than by the structure itself, a replica of a first-century Roman villa.

Paula had always wanted to visit Europe, had even planned once to go with Mickey, but at the last minute he wagered on a sure thing—a horse called Trip to France. It finished next to last, taking their vacation money with it.

Tom navigated a private road leading down toward the ocean. A security guard checked their names against a list and gave them directions.

The house sprawled below them on a secluded lot. As they wound down the drive, Paula spotted a group of people standing out front on the beach.

"Are we late?" she said. "What time is it?"

"Almost ten. Perfect."

The Jensens strolled up the slope to greet them, two other couples trailing behind. Carl and Mary Samms were about the Jensens' age, as was the owner of the house, Jimmy Conrad. But his new bride, a striking redhead named Angela, looked so young that Paula felt old at twenty-seven.

If the men greeted Tom with reserve, there was no such restraint where Paula was concerned. Louise and Mary took her under their wings, shooing her into the kitchen for a glass of iced tea. Angela skipped alongside in her expensive Italian sandals, clearly overjoyed to find someone nearer her own age.

In between listening to bits of conversation about the brush fires and the weather, Paula gazed about with interest. The place was enormous, low and rambling in the Spanish style, with gleaming wooden floors and splashes of Indian weavings on the walls. Lots of wicker furniture, all of it spotless. She was willing to bet Angela didn't do the cleaning.

The young hostess chose the first opportunity to spirit Paula off to her dressing room, on the pretext that they could change into their bathing suits, but more likely to get away from the sedate conversation of the other women.

The dressing room was part of a bedroom suite, with an immense closet running the length of one wall. Paula tried not to show her envy as Angela slid open the closet door to retrieve her beach cover-up, revealing an array of designer dresses with a pack of fur coats at one end.

I'd settle for a mouton collar on one of my cleaning uniforms, Paula thought wryly.

"Don't you just hate this constant talk about business?" asked Angela, stepping unabashedly out of her white slacks and print blouse. "How long have you and Tom been married?"

"Not long," Paula said, removing her own clothes. "How about you?"

"Two months." Angela giggled. "Can you believe this place? I used to be a cocktail waitress. And a good one. Honestly, I'm not ashamed of it."

"I hope not." Paula was tempted to admit having been a cleaning lady herself, but for once better judgment prevailed. She could tell Angela had a loose tongue, and word would surely get back to Jimmy.

The bathing suit Angela selected was a minuscule bikini, in a dark green that brought out the color of her eyes and highlighted the brilliance of her auburn hair. It was easy to see why Jimmy had fallen for her.

Paula had chosen the most conservative swimsuit she possessed, but that wasn't saying much. A deep rose color that flattered her blond hair, it was one piece, but cut so low at the bust that her cleavage showed and so high at the hip that her legs looked three inches longer. The only compensation was the modest pale-pink overblouse she'd brought along.

"That looks great!" Angela gazed at the one-piece swimsuit with frank admiration. "Boy, I'm sure glad this isn't going to be a stuffy weekend like I was expecting. Too bad you guys can't stay over until tomorrow. Your husband's really cute. Isn't this weather awful?"

It didn't take long to realize that Angela's sentences simply tumbled out any which way and one thought didn't necessarily follow another.

I've got to be careful, Paula warned herself as she followed Angela through the house and out a patio door toward the beach. With this nature child around I'm liable to forget myself and say something I'll regret.

A Mexican couple, clad in white uniforms, tended a barbecue grill while the rest of the party sat around on expensive beach furniture.

Louise and Mary had changed into large bathing suits with little flared skirts. The men wore T-shirts over their trunks.

Even as she moved up and automatically greeted the others, Paula couldn't tear her eyes away from Tom where he reclined in a lounge chair, wearing his bathing trunks and a T-shirt. He was perspiring in the heat, and the shirt clung to his chest, outlining sculpted muscles and a tapering waist.

As Paula approached, Tom sat up and offered her a beer, his eyes shining amber in the bright light. She was relieved to see that their host permitted at least this much alcohol.

"Thanks." She sat down in a straight-backed beach chair and smiled at the others. Well, here we are, she thought. Now what?

The women listened patiently while the men discussed sports, cars, and politics. Gradually Paula became aware they were sounding Tom out. No doubt they had left it to their accountants to investigate his business; they were checking to see if he "fit in."

Angela fidgeted in her chair, drinking one diet soda after another. Paula had placed her at twenty-two or twenty-three, much younger than her husband, and wondered if their marriage would last. But then, Paula had been the same age as Mickey, and what good had that done?

"It's hot!" The younger woman stood up and caught her husband's hand. Unlike his two partners, Jimmy had escaped middle-age bulge, and his graying hair gave him an air of distinction. Perhaps marrying him had been Angela's way of finding someone she could lean on. "Let's take a swim."

"Sure, you kids go ahead," said Mr. Jensen with an indulgent wave of the hand. Paula saw Tom's gaze flick across the other men's faces as if gauging their reactions.

"Yes, come on," Jimmy urged. "Angela and I don't want to hog the whole ocean."

"How can we resist an invitation like that?" Tom uncoiled from the lounge chair and pulled the T-shirt over his head.

The sight of his broad, hair-roughened chest glistening with sweat struck Paula as amazingly sensuous. Then she realized she was staring and, embarrassed, unbuttoned her cover-up.

She'd forgotten how revealing the suit was until she saw the way Carl Samms's eyes nearly popped out of his head. He was focused on the tantalizing glimpse of cleavage, while Arthur Jensen, she observed with dismay, was completely absorbed by the sight of her bare hips.

Paula glanced apologetically at the two older women, but they were sunbathing with eyes closed.

Tom's hand caught hers, and he dragged her along the sand. "We'd better hit the water before one of those gentlemen has a heart attack," he murmured.

Angela and Jimmy were already in the ocean, off to one side and clearly absorbed in each other. Paula followed Tom obediently into the mild surf.

"How'm I doing?" She waded thigh-deep into the cool water. "Is this swimsuit too bold?"

"Well, let me see." He confronted her sternly, running his palms up the sides of her bare legs. "Nothing objectionable there."

Before she realized what he was doing, his hands cupped her breasts and the thumbs stroked the sensitive inner edges bared by the low neckline. "No one could object to that," he concluded, brushing her nipples lightly through the stretch fabric, and, unexpectedly, pulling her deeper into the water.

"What do you think you're doing?" Her protests were drowned in the wave that broke over them, and she spluttered furiously.

"Just checking you over." The grin popped up a few feet away, like the Cheshire cat appearing out of nowhere. "You did ask my opinion, you know."

"That wasn't an invitation to paw me! What will your friends think?"

"They'll think my wife and I are still in love after all these . . . months." Tom chuckled, and dived.

Too late, Paula saw what he was up to and tried vainly to splash away. Hands grabbed her legs, a body thrust itself under her, and Tom stood up, lifting her out of the water. Ignoring her shrieks, he spun around several times.

Paula's inhibitions flew away somewhere between the cooling ocean spray and the limitless blue sky. How glorious it was to be free, young, and full of life, and to feel Tom's sturdy shoulders beneath her and the reassuring clamp of his arms about her legs.

By the time he lowered her into the water she had no resistance left, only a passion to match his as he gathered her close and kissed her. Another wave swelled around them, and they might have been two South Sea islanders nude in the water that licked around them unabashedly.

"Right now I wish you really were my wife," Tom muttered. "Loan or no loan, I'd strip that suit right off your lascivious body and make love to you in front of the Jensens and everybody."

"I doubt they'd ever recover," she teased, resting her head against his chest to cover her trembling.

"Yoo-hoo! You folks getting hungry?" Louise Jensen had wandered down to the waterline. "The cook says the shish kebab is ready."

With what grace they could muster, Tom and Paula pulled apart and trudged back to shore. Jimmy and Angela, similarly summoned, didn't look any more enthusiastic as they, too, trailed up the beach.

The food was excellent: marinated steak cubes,

mushrooms, cherry tomatoes, and pineapple chunks, along with potato salad and fresh strawberry pie for dessert.

The only dampening note was the occasional tang of smoke in the air and the darkness of the inland sky.

"Maybe we'd better catch the news." Jimmy leaned over and fiddled with the knobs of a portable TV-radio until an announcer came on.

The two fires had joined into one huge blaze burning dangerously close to the Pacific Coast Highway and Malibu Canyon Road. The highway patrol had temporarily closed both routes.

"Looks like you two may end up spending the night after all," Angela chirped.

Paula felt the blood drain out of her face.

"Oh, dear, I am sorry," said Louise Jensen. "I'd feel terrible if you missed your parents' anniversary dinner."

"It's... it's all right." Paula gulped. "Maybe they'll open the roads in an hour or so."

Jimmy frowned. "Not likely. The fire isn't even partly contained yet. Then there'll be cleanup and massive traffic jams. I'm afraid your best bet is to stay here for the night."

"We've got lots of room!" Angela crowed. "Your parents won't mind."

"It isn't their silver anniversary or anything, is it?" Louise asked worriedly.

"No." Paula didn't like this idea at all. Stay over with Tom?

"Perhaps you'd better call," suggested Mary Samms. "Your parents might be worried."

"That's right," Angela agreed, bouncing to her feet.

"Oh—yes, of course." Paula followed her hostess

into the house. To her dismay, the other woman waited while she placed the call.

Sally answered. "Hello?"

"Hi, Mom, this is Paula!" She coughed before continuing, hoping her roommate caught the hint. "Happy anniversary!"

"Have you gone completely out of your mind?"

Quickly Paula explained about the brush fire, trying to keep in mind that she was supposed to be speaking to her mother.

"I see," said Sally. "Well, let me tell you something: You got yourself into this mess; I'll be very curious to see how you get out of it."

"I knew you'd understand, Mom." Paula couldn't repress the sarcastic edge to her voice. "Hope you and Pop have a wonderful time, and we'll see you tomorrow."

"Who knows?" Sally said. "Maybe he'll carry you off to Hong Kong. Or the two of you will ride home on an elephant. Or we'll get to keep the account. Anything could happen."

"Bye, Mom." Paula hung up. "She . . . um . . . was a little upset, but I'm sure she'll be all right."

"Probably just worried about the fire," said Angela as they walked to her dressing room to pick out some clothes for Paula to borrow.

Their next stop was the room. Paula and Tom's room. A large, bright chamber with a queen-size brass bed and French provincial furniture, opening through a glass door onto its own private courtyard.

"Great for sunbathing in the nude." Angela grinned. "Jimmy and his first wife had a big, dark, gloomy house in San Francisco. About two years after she died, he came down here and bought this, and boy, am I glad!"

"It's great," Paula agreed, giving the room one last despairing look. She'd been hoping for twin beds or at least a couch to sleep on, but there was no such luck.

Tom had better behave himself, she thought determinedly as they strolled back to the beach. And so had I.

CHAPTER *Three*

ONCE PAULA ACCEPTED the fact that she was stuck in Malibu for the night, the afternoon and evening passed pleasantly.

They had scarcely recovered from lunch before dinner was served, prime rib with baked potatoes and broccoli. Afterward the couples played cards, husbands and wives separated at two tables.

"It's a lucky thing for us that you had to stay," Mary pointed out. "Otherwise we'd have had six for cards, and that doesn't work no matter how you divide it."

Although point totals were kept, Paula noted there was no money at stake. Clearly the group didn't believe in gambling, a sentiment she heartily endorsed. She couldn't help seeing the irony, though, of refusing to bet on cards while gambling huge sums of money on companies like Clinton Computers.

The conversation remained general, sparing Paula the necessity of telling any more lies. The radio kept them posted as the winds died down and fire crews slowly began to tame the massive blaze.

Bedtime was ten o'clock, but Paula felt wide awake as she and Tom retired to their chamber.

"I apologize for the inconvenience," he told her as she snatched Angela's nightie and robe from a hook and headed for the bathroom. "You don't seriously believe I started the brush fire just to get us stranded here, do you?"

"No." Paula turned and regarded him, standing there with arms loosely folded across his broad chest and a teasing look in those tan eyes. "But I could still get burned."

Burned wasn't a strong enough word. Scorched, she thought as she locked herself in the bathroom. Char-broiled. Fried to a crisp.

She hung Angela's borrowed dress on a hook and slipped on the nightgown.

Oops. The silky pink material edged generously with lace had appeared modest enough on the hanger. Somehow it didn't look the same draped over Paula's curves. In fact, it looked downright transparent. Quickly she topped it with the matching negligee. That wasn't much better.

Paula stuck her head out the door. Tom was standing right there, waiting.

"Go away," she hissed.

"Where would you suggest?"

"Maybe you could stick your head in the closet until I'm tucked in. Angela's clothes are made out of cellophane." She fixed him with a steely look, which had about as much effect as attacking a killer whale with a squirt gun.

"I promise to behave myself, but there's no harm in looking," Tom replied.

"Then I'm staying in the bathroom." Paula started

to shut the door, but Tom caught it and wedged his shoulder in the crack.

"This isn't the way sophisticated people behave," he said as she pushed furiously and fruitlessly. "Haven't you ever watched old Cary Grant movies?"

"I'm not sophisticated," she snapped. "I never claimed to be. I'm the cleaning lady, remember? Oh, how did I ever get myself into this mess?"

"Let's compromise," said Tom. "You come out. I go in. You get into bed. I get into bed. Then we both go to sleep."

Paula stopped pushing and thought it over. "Couldn't you sleep on the floor? The carpet looks thick enough."

"And when I can't walk tomorrow because my muscles have gridlocked, how am I going to explain that to our hosts?"

She was about to insist when she remembered that Tom was her boss. Maybe she should sleep on the floor.

It didn't sound very comfortable, Paula thought grimly. But they said hard surfaces were good for backaches. She'd been having a lot of these lately, from her cleaning work.

"I won't do anything you don't want me to do," Tom added innocently.

There didn't seem to be any alternative. "Okay. But if you get fresh with me I'll scream."

"I believe you."

She opened the door and glared at him. Tom whistled. She slammed the door.

Now what? She couldn't stay here all night.

Paula glanced around desperately. A bath towel! She wrapped one tightly around herself, over the negligee. It looked ridiculous, but at least it was opaque.

Thus safely covered, she exited and, ignoring Tom's disbelieving grimace, crawled into the far side of the bed.

She could follow his movements from the sound of running water and brushing noises. Listening to a man get ready for bed was almost more intimate than actually watching him, she reflected.

True to his word, Tom made no move toward her as he slipped between the covers and snapped off the light. Within minutes his breathing became regular and deep.

Paula lay huddled as close to the edge of the bed as she could without falling out. She hadn't shared a bed with a man since she and Mickey split up.

How she'd put up with her husband for five years was more than she could comprehend. No, that's not true, she scolded herself. You closed your mind to what you didn't want to know.

It was the down payment for the house that struck the final blow. A trip to Europe, dearly as she longed for it, was only a dream, but the house had been the first step toward starting a family. When Mickey blew the money in one drunken weekend, she saw with sudden certainty that there was never going to be any magic number or any ship that came in. Only disappointment after disappointment until they despised each other and themselves.

The thought of how far she'd come from that awful moment soothed Paula's nerves, and she fell asleep.

A while later, she drifted upward to consciousness. Something was weighing her down . . . her calves. . . . A leg. Tom's leg, thrown across her as he tossed.

Paula shifted uncomfortably, wondering how to

extricate herself without waking him. A part of her didn't really want to. The best moments with Mickey had been the natural intimacy that a man and woman share when they touch each other unintentionally in the course of living, eating, resting together. It felt safe and reassuring now to know Tom was there beside her.

Somewhere in the middle of these musings, Paula dozed off again.

She blinked her eyes open. Sunlight flooded the room through the open glass doors, and in the secluded courtyard she could see a male figure stretched out on a towel.

Hmph. Mornings were not her best time.

Paula yawned and glanced down at the rumpled bed. It was amazing that somehow she'd survived the night lying right next to Tom Clinton.

Pushing aside the covers, she touched her bare feet to the carpet and stretched. She was too unawake to feel self-conscious, her face still softly childlike with sleep, her blond hair an appealingly shaggy mane, the sunlight clarifying the contours of her body through the thin nightgown.

"Good morning," Tom called. "Brunch isn't until half past ten, but there's a pot of coffee and some pastry on the bureau."

Rewrapping herself in the protective towel, Paula reached toward the nightstand and then remembered her watch was still at the jeweler's. "What time is it?"

"Nine-thirty. Plenty of time to get a tan." He grinned lazily and rolled over onto his stomach.

The coffee was hot in its insulated container. Paula tore off half a lemon Danish and munched it as she sat cross-legged on the bed.

Yes, I would like to live like this, she thought, her eyes straying over the muscular expanse of Tom's back and the taut rounded shape of his buttocks. But life isn't a weekend at the beach.

She sighed, dusted the crumbs carefully into the waste basket, and got up.

Her swimsuit had dried off from the previous day. Paula inspected herself to see if the feasting had expanded her flat stomach, but so far she saw no effects. Might as well pig out: it would be hot dogs and baked beans again on Monday.

The day was mild this early, and the sunlight felt good on her shoulders as she spread out a towel next to Tom.

"Paula?" He lifted his head and squinted at her. "Would you put on my suntan lotion? It's right there."

"Okay." She picked up the bottle and, with only a moment's hesitation, squirted it across his back. Reaching out tentatively, she smoothed it over his skin. "Is this what you expect from your employees?"

"Only the women. You're not doing that right, you know. It has to be rubbed in."

"Well, excuse me!" She swung one leg over him and thumped down astraddle, knocking the wind out of him.

"Didn't anyone ever teach you how to treat a man?" he demanded.

"Yes. My roommate. She said, 'Kick 'em where it hurts.'" Paula leaned forward and spread the lotion across his shoulders. His skin was hot. "You didn't really want suntan lotion, you wanted another sample of my massaging."

"That's right."

Paula's fingers dug around the edges of his shoulder blades, and his muscles yielded.

The sensuous feel of his skin made her senses more acute. She became aware of the background rumble of the ocean and the mewing of seabirds; the tantalizing smell of suntan lotion mixed with sun-heated flesh; the firmness of his body beneath and between her thighs.

Now, that was thinking dangerously.

Paula applied herself with renewed vigor until the last of the lotion disappeared.

"Done." She climbed off and stretched out, face down, on her own towel.

"Turnabout's fair play." He flung a leg over her and sat astride. A cold stream of lotion sprayed onto Paula's back, and she gasped.

Strong fingers caught the nape of her neck and pressed. She hadn't even been aware of the stiffness until he found it. As his hands splayed across her back, kneading and probing, her resistance evaporated. Sun-heat and body heat combined to melt her bones.

Tom found the hidden kinks in her arm muscles, the slight remaining tension along her spine. He slipped off the bra straps, and Paula made no protest.

Now his explorations moved down her sides, and Paula felt his lips graze the nape of her neck. "Is this part of applying the lotion?"

"The best part." He lifted himself off her and stretched out at her side, turning her so they faced. "Didn't you know the lips are the most heavily muscled part of your body?"

"No, I didn't."

"Neither did I, but let's find out if it's true." His

mouth traced across hers temptingly, the pressure increasing gradually as he claimed her lips, tongue, inner cheeks, teeth.

Without interrupting the kiss, he rolled Paula onto her back and bent over her. She found her tongue twisting against his, her hands catching his shoulders.

He looked up. "Proved my point?"

"About what?"

"Lips. I see I haven't. Well, let's try this." He brushed his mouth down her throat, the tip of his tongue leaving a path of desire.

He nuzzled the inner curve of her shoulders, tasted the sun-sweet expanse of skin across her collarbone. Vaguely Paula noted that her straps had slipped lower, that the deep slash of the neckline had parted to reveal the upper swell of her breasts. A yearning to feel his tantalizing mouth against the hidden nipples surged through her like a power volt.

Instead, Tom returned his mouth to her own. Paula clutched him, tucking herself half under him as she responded to his lovemaking. Somewhere a voice murmured a warning, but the crackle of electricity between them drowned it out.

Tom lifted his head and gazed down at her flushed face. Then, at last, he peeled down the swimsuit to expose the straining pink tips of her breasts. His breath warmed across them, and then his tongue licked delicately. Paula closed her eyes, lost in sensation.

With a groan, his control slipped away. He caught her breasts firmly between his hands, twin peaks bared beneath his mastery. There was no restraint to the way his mouth dominated her, sucking, squeezing, demanding.

Fire. She was on fire. Her body had a will of its

own, thrusting against him, urging him on.

She could feel his masculine readiness through their swimsuits. The reality of what would come next struck her like an ocean wave. Loving with Tom would be intense, intense and binding. Binding on her, but not on him. She hardly knew the man. Hardly knew herself, at this moment.

Paula pulled away, confused and a little frightened. If she could yield this readily, how would it be afterward?

Everything. She'd give him everything; stinginess wasn't in her nature. And then? Even if he loved her, he was as much a gambler in his own way as Mickey had been in his. No room for the family and the security she wanted so much.

"What's the matter?" Tom's mouth twisted as he watched her.

"I . . . I'm sorry. I lost control." She pulled up the bathing suit, covering herself. "I didn't mean to lead you on."

"Why stop?" he said. "We're both adults. And I assure you, I'm not the shallow type who gets bored with a woman as soon as she goes to bed with him."

"I know." Paula sat up and hugged her knees. "It's more than that."

A polite rap at the bedroom door interrupted them. "Yes?" Tom called.

"Brunch in fifteen minutes, Mr. Clinton," came a female voice.

"Thanks." He fixed Paula with a stern look. "I'm not giving up. Consider this a brief reprieve." He stood, gathered his towel, and headed into the bathroom.

Not giving up? Paula shook her head. They'd be going back to Anaheim today, and the game would be over. She would return to being the cleaning lady, and Tom would be once again the unapproachable millionaire whose manager had employed her.

As she paced into the bedroom and dressed quickly in her shorts and halter top, Paula felt a stab of regret. She'd never felt this fully alive with a man before, even Mickey. And now it was going to end almost before it began.

Tom said nothing further until the two of them joined the others for a splendid brunch of sausage, eggs, melon slices, freshly baked rolls, and coffee. Then he made easy conversation, as if nothing had happened.

The radio announced that the roads were clear. They left about one o'clock after a warm farewell from the other couples.

"Do you think it went all right?" Paula asked as they headed east along the Pacific Coast Highway. "Are you going to get the loan?"

"Arthur said he'd give me a call later in the week." Tom kept his eyes on the road. "It seems they have a silent partner, and he has to approve the deal, too. But it looks good."

"I'm glad," Paula said. "Maybe I even helped?"

He spared her a ghost of a smile. "You definitely helped. They apparently didn't feel comfortable dealing socially with a single male, but I was welcome as half of a couple. And everyone liked you."

"I hope so." They were through the town now, and inland Paula noticed black scars across the hills. The fires were part of a natural cycle, clearing the way for new growth, but their periodic rampages frightened her nevertheless.

"How long were you married?" Tom asked unexpectedly.

"Five years."

"I think you have some burn marks of your own," he said. "What was your husband like?"

"He gambled." That said everything: the obsession, the lying, the roller coaster of hope and disappointment.

Tom nodded. "So do I."

"I know."

"It's part of life, Paula. It's part of the way I am. Not two-bit betting on horses, but big stuff." He glanced at her as if trying to read her reaction.

"That's fine. For you. But I've had enough of it." She rested her head against the door, feeling the whirr of the engine vibrate through her.

"Oh, I'm not so sure," Tom said. "I think it's in your blood, too, whether you like it or not."

She didn't answer. Paula frequently ran risks, and usually paid for them dearly. All the more reason to look for someone she could depend on.

It was after two when they arrived in Anaheim, and Paula declined an invitation to come up for a drink.

"Got to go," she said. "It's been fun."

Tom's voice floated after her as she jerked open her car door. "I'll be seeing you, Paula."

Sure, she reminded herself. On Friday. When I come to clean the apartment.

Was he going to pursue her, shower her with gifts and tempt her with fancy dinners and theater tickets? Paula sighed. It would be hard to pass up such luxuries after the penny-pinching life she'd led since the divorce. But far more than that, it would be hard to keep her arms and lips and heart from welcoming Tom.

You dummy, she told herself. You're just asking for trouble.

She gave herself a mental shake and buttressed her resolve as she parked next to her apartment building.

There was no word from Tom, not on Monday or Tuesday or Wednesday. The only relief was that, after a few sardonic comments, Sally dropped the subject.

Paula found herself dreading Friday, when she'd be cleaning the penthouse. Would Tom be there? What would he say? How would she react? She didn't dare ask Sally to swap tasks with her, knowing that would stir up her roommate's sarcasm all over again.

Thursdays were devoted to cleaning a small industrial building. It was almost six o'clock when Paula staggered wearily back to the apartment, a box of take-out fried chicken tucked under her arm.

Sally was sitting in the living room wearing a smug expression.

"What's going on?" Paula called from the kitchen as she dumped the box on the table and washed her hands.

"You had a call." Sally came to stand in the doorway. "Tom Clinton says he's looking foward to seeing you tomorrow."

"He called to say that?" Paula shook her head. "Have you eaten yet? We could split this."

"I had a hamburger already." From the look on her face, Sally hadn't finished describing Tom's call.

"And?" Paula transferred the contents of the box onto a plate.

"And he wants you there at seven-thirty in the morning."

"Why so early?"

"He has a special job for you." Sally couldn't repress a smirk. "For about five days. He said he'll pay for a temporary replacement, your expenses, and a hundred dollars a day for your time."

Paula regarded her roommate suspiciously. "What does he want me to do for the money?"

"He described it as a mop-up operation," said Sally.

"Tom Clinton can do his own mopping up," snapped Paula. "Who does he think he is?"

Sally was still grinning, maddeningly. "I don't think you're going to turn this one down. But there is one requirement."

"What?"

"You have to bring your passport." Sally savored Paula's confusion before adding, "He's taking you to Paris."

CHAPTER
Four

ON FRIDAY MORNING, Paula found a space in the Clinton Computers parking lot. She sat in the car for a moment, debating.

In the trunk was her packed suitcase. In her purse was the passport she'd obtained for the trip to Europe that she and Mickey never took.

But should she go?

It was hard to resist a chance to visit Paris, especially when the offer came practically paved in gold. Even Sally had seemed to approve. But Paula had a feeling this was going to be another crazy scheme, and she wasn't sure she wanted any part of it. Especially not if it meant staying close to Tom Clinton. She knew the limits of her own strength.

Well, the least she could do was go inside and find out what he was up to.

Leaving the suitcase, she slid out of the car and joined the crowd of office workers heading into the building. How different it looked today, full of people and light, not isolated and spooky as it had on Sunday.

The elevator was packed, which meant it was closer

to eight o'clock than seven-thirty. With the money Tom would be paying her, she could finally get her watch out of hock. If she accepted.

In twos and threes, the others got off on lower floors. Paula rode up from the eleventh floor to the twelfth by herself.

She marched down the short hallway to the apartment. Although she had a key, it seemed wiser to ring.

From inside, Tom's voice called, "Come in." Paula turned the doorknob and entered. There was no one in the living room.

"I'm in here." The bedroom.

She went to stand in the doorway. At the double closet, Tom was hanging suits inside a garment bag.

"Going somewhere?" she asked.

He turned in surprise. "Didn't your roommate tell you? You did bring your passport, I hope."

Paula folded her arms defiantly. "I don't even know what this is about. What makes you think that all you have to do is snap your fingers and I'll jump?"

A beautiful navy silk jacket joined the other clothes in the garment bag before Tom turned and grinned. "I'm not snapping my fingers; I'm jingling my cash register."

"I may be poor, but I'm not for sale."

Tom stepped away from the closet and inspected her. "Have I told you yet that you look terrific?"

The rose linen dress with matching jacket was the product of one of Mickey's spending sprees, and Paula knew it looked good on her. But the compliment made her suspicious. "Why do you want to take me to Paris?"

"Because I think it would be terrifically romantic to make love to you in the Bois de Boulogne." He lifted her hand and kissed the back of it tenderly. In spite of herself, Paula felt a shiver of pleasure.

Being romanced in Paris sounded a darn sight better than mucking out industrial buildings. But...

"This has something to do with the loan, doesn't it?" she said.

"Oh, did I forget to mention that?" His mouth quirked with amusement. "Yes, as a matter of fact. It seems the Jensens *et al.* have a silent partner in Paris. A financier by the name of Jacques d'Armand. He wants to meet Mr. and Mrs. Clinton personally."

"Couldn't he just meet Mr. Clinton?"

"It wouldn't have the same effect." Tom still held her hand, but his expression sobered. "I do need your help, Paula. Just play the game the way you did in Malibu. You'll have a paid vacation and a free tour of Paris. Have you had a better offer recently?"

It did sound tempting. More than tempting. Irresistible.

"When would we leave?" she said.

"The plane takes off from Los Angeles International in a little over two hours, which in rush hour traffic means we're cutting it close." Tom moved away to zip up the garment bag. "Where's your stuff?"

"Downstairs in the car."

"A gift." From his pocket, he produced a small black jeweler's box.

Paula opened it to find a magnificent wedding ring, set with a diamond and half a dozen emeralds. It fit a bit loosely, but not enough to be a problem. This wasn't part of the deal he'd told Sally about, and she didn't like to think what he expected in return.

"I'd rather consider this a loan," she said.

"If you like. Now let's get moving." He picked up

his luggage and led the way out of the penthouse.

Before she knew it, Paula found herself standing at the airline check-in desk, digging out her passport for the ticket agent.

"A virgin," Tom said, observing the pristine pages where no visas had been stamped.

"Yes, poor thing," Paula rejoined. The woman behind the counter didn't bat an eye as she finished her paperwork.

They passed through security and reached the waiting room as the plane was beginning to board. "By the way," Paula said, "what are we going to do about names?"

"Names?"

"On our passports. Didn't it occur to you that this Mr. d'Armand might happen to see them?"

"He probably won't. If he does, we'll say you kept your maiden name. Professionally." He certainly knew how to lie quickly and glibly, Paula thought. Just like Mickey.

Tom led the way along an enclosed ramp into the plane. A stewardess glanced at their boarding passes and directed them to the front.

First class? Paula smiled with delight, then returned to more serious matters. "But what do you mean, professionally? I thought I only did volunteer work."

"You didn't actually tell anyone that, right? Let's make you a writer. But only if someone asks. No point in borrowing trouble."

Paula thought this over as she settled into her seat by the window. "You're good at this." As she spoke, she fumbled with her seat belt. It was stuck between the seats, and she tugged at it futilely.

"Allow me." Tom worked the belt free, then leaned

over and fastened it about her waist. His hands lingered longer than necessary.

"Is this part of the job?" Paula asked to disguise the unbidden excitement in her stomach. She hoped France didn't have a quarantine on butterflies or she'd be in big trouble.

"We need to appear affectionate. For authenticity's sake." He tipped her chin up and caught her mouth with his before she could protest. The kiss was quick but thorough, and by the time Tom lifted his head away he'd proven he could melt her knees at will. Fortunately she was sitting down, so he couldn't tell.

It was a long flight to New York, then a change of planes and an even longer flight across the Atlantic. At least Paula didn't have to bother about setting her watch ahead, since she didn't have one.

Paris, she thought sleepily, leaning her head against Tom's conveniently placed shoulder. The Eiffel Tower. The Louvre. Tom Clinton.

What sort of circles did this Jacques d'Armand move in? It occurred to her somewhere east of Newfoundland that her wardrobe scarcely befitted the wife of an American millionaire. Some of her shoes were downright ratty; there was one pair of fake patent leather pumps whose cracks she'd colored in with black felt-tip marker.

"Tom?" she murmured. "What if I don't have the right clothes?"

"If there's any doubt, take them off," he said. "I guarantee that no red-blooded Frenchman will hold it against you."

She bit his arm.

The flight droned on. Somehow they both managed to doze. It was a short night, with the hours peeling away at double their usual rate, and Paula awoke feeling as if she needed a week at a health spa. Tom, on the other hand, snapped into consciousness clear-eyed and alert. Ready for the upcoming challenge.

Paula observed surreptitiously how he spoke politely with the stewardess, requesting and receiving an advance on their coffee. In the same circumstances, Mickey would have chatted with the woman at length, flaunting his charm until it frayed around the edges.

During the next hour, Tom shepherded Paula to the exit the moment the plane landed, retrieved their luggage before anyone else, and sailed through customs with an air of detached courtesy that disarmed the inspectors.

A man walked toward them, making eye contact with Tom. He was thirtyish and bland, like the Secret Service agents she'd seen on television flanking the President.

This, she quickly learned, was not the mysterious Jacques d'Armand but his assistant, whose name sounded like an incomprehensible mumble. Speaking in English, he escorted them to a chauffeured limousine.

They took a freeway, which he called an *autoroute*. Paula peered into the distance, hoping for a glimpse of the Eiffel Tower, but they were skirting the city.

She glanced at Tom to see if he'd noted her disappointment, but his attention was focused entirely on M. d'Armand's assistant, of whom he asked a few well-chosen questions.

I'd better get my tour of Paris or there are going to be feathers flying, Paula vowed silently before settling back in her seat to contemplate the French countryside.

Finally the chauffeur turned through a stone gate into a private drive. The road led upward through a grassy park. Ahead of them, behind some trees, Paula caught a glimpse of stone turrets. She forgot her disappointment at missing the city.

"The chateau dates back to the fourteenth century, although it was partly destroyed by fire and rebuilt in the eighteenth," said d'Armand's assistant.

They cleared the trees, and the mansion spread before them, four stories high and sprawling across enough ground for a couple of hotels. Paula had never seen anything like it outside of a movie.

"Most impressive," Tom said. "There must be quite a staff on the premises."

Spoken like a millionaire, she thought admiringly. And he had a point. Looking at the enormous house, she could understand now why noblemen had those upstairs and downstairs maids.

They mounted the broad stone steps and entered a hall that resembled the waiting room in Grand Central Station. In fact, d'Armand's aide noted, the front rooms, with their carved ceilings and marble floors, were sometimes opened for public viewing.

Instinctively, Paula clung to Tom's arm as they proceeded into the ancient elevator, its open grillwork giving them an unsettlingly clear view of the creaky machinery.

M. and Mme. d'Armand were in town, but would be returning shortly, the assistant assured them as he ushered them to their room on the third floor. Unfortunately they would not be able to meet the two teenage daughters; the elder, Giselle, was on the French equestrian team, and the younger, Marie-Louise, was vacationing in Switzerland with friends.

Tom thanked the man for his help while Paula gazed about their quarters in delight.

The chamber was enormous, with a fireplace at one side and thick carpets underfoot. She took in the oversize four-poster bed, the gleaming wooden wardrobes that served as closets, the subtle wallpaper with its fleur-de-lis pattern, and the elaborate chandelier.

Striding across the room to open the French windows, she found herself on a balcony that ran the length of the room. It overlooked a garden, bright splashes of flowers bordering the walkways and roses climbing about an arched trellis.

"This place is magnificent." She inhaled deeply.

Tom came to stand behind her, draped his arms about her waist and rested his cheek against her hair. "Would you like to live in a house like this?"

"As long as I didn't have to clean it." She leaned back against him and closed her eyes, enjoying his nearness and the faint fragrance from the garden. "But I'd settle for a comfortable little California bungalow."

A wave of weariness swept over her, mingled with a deep sense of peace. She had the strangest feeling that with Tom's arms around her, she would have felt at home anywhere.

"Tired?" he murmured.

"Uh-huh."

Tom drew her toward the bed and turned back the quilt. "You look like someone just switched off your light."

"I know. I feel as if my arms and legs are weighed down with chains," she admitted, sinking onto the edge of the bed and wondering how she would get the wrinkles out of her clothes if she slept in them.

"I'm too tired to undress."

"Can't let my wife down, can I?" Mischievously, he drew off her jacket, then unzipped her dress. Too groggy to protest, Paula let him pull it off and watched as he hung it and the jacket in a wardrobe. She felt like a child being prepared for sleep.

Her shoes slid free by themselves, but Tom knelt and carefully unrolled her pantyhose. His fingers smoothed against her legs, and he planted a light kiss on the inside of her thigh before removing the stockings and draping them over the back of a chair.

Paula trembled deliciously. Inside, a voice warned, You aren't really married, you know.

She gazed at Tom through her shaggy blond hair, sleepily aware that she was clad only in an enticing pink slip. She ought to cover up, ought to decry his boldness . . .

"Are you still awake?" he teased.

"I'm not sure."

"Let's find out." Tom sat beside her and buried his face against her neck. His mouth found the hollow of her throat, then proceeded slowly downward.

Suddenly he stopped and drew back. "You're asleep," he said.

"Yes, but I have romantic dreams," she heard herself say.

A moment of silence. Somehow Paula pried her eyelids open wide enough to look at him. He was studying her with an almost savage expression.

"You don't know how much I'd like to take advantage of you." A guttural note roughened his voice. "But when I make love to you, Paula, you're going to be awake for every minute of it."

Once again he kissed her and stroked his hand

across the unresisting softness of her stomach. She felt him pull the covers over her, and then the mattress sprang up where Tom's weight had been.

She wanted to call him back. She wanted to argue that she needed the warmth of him in her arms. But she had already fallen asleep.

Bubbles. Paula was dreaming of bubbles. Tangy bits of froth blew against her skin and into her nose. It tickled, and she turned her head against the pillow and sneezed.

"That's no way to treat good champagne."

Tom's comment dragged her into the real world. It was evening, Paula realized with dismay; the drapes were drawn and the chandelier overhead cast a soft glow over the room. She'd napped through her first day in France.

"You shouldn't have let me sleep so long!" she protested, taking the glass Tom had been waving under her nose. "Where've you been?"

"Our host is back." He picked up his own glass from the nightstand and clinked it against hers. "To success."

"To honesty." She took a sip. It really was good champagne, and it tasted wonderful in her dry mouth. The airplane had left her feeling parched.

"Monsieur and Madame d'Armand request the honor of our company at a party they're hosting tonight," Tom continued. "It'll give us a chance to meet some of their acquaintances, and of course, it'll let him see us in a social setting."

"Him?" she said. "Doesn't Madame d'Armand get any say in the matter?"

"My sources tell me Jacques is a traditionalist—

rigidly so, which is why he must never suspect the truth about our relationship." There was nothing light-hearted about Tom now. "So be on your best behavior, Paula."

Work. Well, that was what the trip was about, and she was being well paid. "Any advice?"

"Yes." Tom took away her empty goblet. "You may have no more than two additional glasses of champagne during the evening, and nothing else alcoholic to drink. The last thing we need is for either of us to get tipsy."

About to take offense, Paula felt her annoyance subside at the last remark. At least he was including himself.

"Who'll be here?" She sat up, wrapping a sheet around herself. "They must be horribly rich. I really don't have the right clothes."

"Too bad you can't wear your lingerie. It's smashing." Tom grinned. "Or were you suggesting that I take you shopping?"

Paula glared at him. "I was not! I'm merely trying to do my job to the best of my ability." How could he believe she'd expect a man to buy her expensive presents?

Or maybe that was how he related to women—paying them for services rendered. Well, there weren't going to be any services, she thought determinedly, except for this charade, which couldn't end too soon for her taste.

"Just wear something simple and classy." He didn't seem to notice her reaction. "No one expects anything of you but that you behave with grace and listen with interest to the conversation. The spotlight will be on me."

"Fine." Her chin resting on her knees, Paula regarded Tom.

How little she knew him. Sometimes she felt as if they were old friends, even a real married couple. Then a word, a gesture, a fleeting expression would remind her that this was a ruthlessly ambitious man who didn't hesitate to deceive in order to get what he wanted.

"Tom," she said, "what we're doing—it isn't really unethical, is it? I mean, you're not trying to cheat the man, are you?"

"A little late for pangs of conscience, wouldn't you say?" He stood, and Paula noticed that he'd changed into a fresh suit. "But no, all I'm doing is seeking a loan. And straightening out the mess you got me into when you showed up half-naked in my bedroom."

"What time is it?"

"Almost seven. They'll be serving a buffet downstairs in a few minutes. If you're hungry, that is."

She discovered that she was ravenous.

A light blue dress with a scoop neck seemed to fit Tom's requirements, she decided a few minutes later. She glanced at the armchair where he sat reading an English-language newspaper, but he paid no attention.

Her hair presented the usual problem. Tired of pushing it out of her eyes, Paula brushed it back and secured it with a silver semicircular band she'd bought months before but never used. The effect was startlingly sophisticated. The hair lay flat against her head close to her face, focusing attention on her large blue eyes. Then, behind the band, the hair fluffed out into a mane.

Paula applied makeup and, studying herself, was pleased to see that—hopefully!—she looked the part of a society lady.

"Well?" she said.

Tom set down the newspaper. For a moment he kept silent, and Paula thought with a sinking sensation that she'd botched things. Then he let out a low wolf whistle.

"You'll knock 'em dead." He rose and offered her his arm. "Come along, beautiful woman."

She slid her arm through his, and they stepped into the hall. Ready or not, Mrs. Thomas C. Clinton III was about to meet the world.

CHAPTER
Five

THE BUFFET WAS set out in a gleaming dining room on the second floor, which was evidently where the d'Armands did their entertaining. Paula estimated the crowd at about a hundred and fifty people, mostly middle-aged or older and expensively garbed in what looked like designer originals. The most stunning of all was a tall blond woman in a flowing chiffon gown. Regal without looking in the least pretentious, she moved through the assembly like a ballerina.

"Simone d'Armand," Tom murmured. "She used to be an actress—and a very good one, I hear—before she gave it up for marriage."

A silver-haired man turned toward them, and instantly Paula knew he must be Jacques d'Armand. Although only of average height, he had an arresting appearance, his gray hair contrasting markedly with the tanned skin and keen alertness. She guessed him to be in his early forties, and would have been willing to bet that he knew precisely what was going on in each corner of the room at any given moment... including every gesture his wife made.

D'Armand caught sight of them, and Paula felt his appraising stare as he nodded to his wife and then strode in their direction.

"Madame Clinton, I am so pleased to meet you. I was sorry to miss you earlier, but your husband said you were sleeping." His gaze swept over her in assessment, and Paula was glad she'd worn a conservative dress.

"Your home is lovely," she responded. "Thank you for inviting us."

Simone d'Armand reached them and introductions were made. "Please come and eat," she said, speaking English with a charming hint of an accent. "You've had a long journey."

The two women walked together to the buffet. The food was splendid—lobster and crab, pâté and a selection of cheeses—but Paula was more interested in the hostess.

Simone's well-modulated voice soothed across Paula's senses even when the woman turned to speak to someone in French. No need to understand the words to know that here was an expert in the fine art of staying in the background and making guests feel welcome.

Paula wondered if women were a mere adjunct when it came to doing business in France, or was that the case only in this household? Jacques struck her as the kind of man who liked to keep his life under tight control.

Tom wasn't eating, she noticed. Perhaps he felt that holding a plate would hinder his handshaking—he was certainly doing enough of that as Jacques conducted him around the room.

As she tasted the crab, Paula watched Tom admiringly. Each time he was introduced to a new circle, men nodded respectfully and women looked him over closely.

"So." Simone guided Paula to a couch. "You are newlyweds, I hear."

Paula nodded. Somehow it was harder to lie to this exquisite, gentle woman than to anyone else she'd met.

"How romantic, to come to France—but not so much, perhaps, for financial matters," her hostess reflected. "Do you have your own work also?"

Paula pretended to be occupied swallowing her food before giving the answer Tom had coached. "I do some writing occasionally."

"Ah, but nothing that interferes with your duties to your husband?" Simone looked thoughtful. "But that is not always the way with American women?"

"We . . . certainly have a lot of independence." Was her hostess being critical, or was that a note of envy in her voice? "My husband mentioned that you used to be an actress. I wish I could have seen you perform."

A shadow crossed Simone's lovely face. "It was a splendid time for me, to be so young and free. But, of course, it has been wonderful having my beautiful daughters. I only wish you could meet them."

No mention of her husband, Paula noted. She was searching for some innocuous reply when the men returned. At the same time, she heard strains of waltz music wafting in through the doorway.

"We hope you ladies will join us for the dancing," Jacques said, bowing low.

Tom held out his arm to Paula. She set aside her empty plate and stood, slipping her hand into the crook of his elbow and basking in the glow of his smile.

At the same time, she couldn't help noticing how stiffly Simone took her husband's arm, as impersonally as if he were an usher at a wedding. Already, the hostess was focusing her attention on her guests, urging them to move to the next room.

"You're making quite a hit," Tom murmured. "You seem to have established quite a rapport with our hostess."

"I like her," Paula admitted.

"Just don't get too close," he cautioned. "Remember the old wartime slogan: Loose lips sink ships."

They followed the others into the next room, not exactly a ballroom, but certainly a space designed for entertaining, with handsome gilded couches grouped for easy conversation and a large area left clear for dancing. The orchestra, seated in one corner, bristled with violins. No rock 'n' roll here.

"By the way," Tom said, keeping his voice low, "do you dance?"

"Sure." Ballroom dancing had been the one hobby she and Mickey shared, and Paula looked forward to showing that in one area at least she could match the other guests for elegance.

Tom swung her onto the floor. At a nightclub, couples might sway languidly together, but tonight Tom and Paula kept slightly apart for propriety's sake as they whirled lightly around the dance floor.

The touch of Tom's hand on her waist sent warm tingles through Paula. Their bodies moved in unison, as if they'd danced together many times.

He felt...right. He knew just when to swing her around, how to hold her firmly without grasping, where to guide her so they never bumped anyone.

To her disappointment, the waltz ended and it was time to go back to work.

With Paula beside him, Tom moved skillfully from group to group. Most of the time she could only listen as the conversation peaked and eddied in French, but she kept a bright smile on her face.

Many of the women made an attempt to talk with her in halting English. Paula found that with hand gestures and lots of good will, she was able to communicate fairly well.

Jacques, circulating among the crowd, stopped at her side. "You dance beautifully," he said. "You do so often, in America?"

"Not nearly as much as I'd like," She glanced over at her make-believe husband, but he merely shot her an encouraging smile and continued his conversation. "Tom generally avoids public places, as you probably know."

"Ah, yes. That is why no one knew he had married," he said.

Paula didn't detect any suspicion in the words, but she found their host's nearness disturbing. Those intense gray eyes didn't miss much.

The orchestra finished a samba and launched into another waltz. "Would you do me the honor of dancing with me?" Jacques inquired.

"Yes, I'd love to."

It felt strange, after her whirl with Tom, to be walking onto the dance floor with this stranger. But Paula managed a smile as Jacques's hand came to rest on her waist.

He danced with fluid grace, and Paula found herself following easily, although there was none of the electricity that had sparked between her and Tom.

Instinctively, she glanced around until she spotted Simone. Mme. d'Armand was speaking with a waiter, gesturing at the tray of empty champagne glasses he carried, and Paula gathered that her attention was occupied by the logistics of running the event smoothly.

Entertaining was Simone's job. No wonder the hostess didn't appear to mind that her husband was waltzing with a succession of other women. This wasn't really a social occasion for them, not any more than it was for Tom and Paula.

"You have been to France before?" Jacques asked politely.

"No," Paula said. "I meant to come once . . ." She'd nearly mentioned her ex-husband! "But now that I'm here, I'm enchanted."

"How kind of you." Jacques smiled. "Considering that you have seen only a little countryside and my house."

"Well, everything I've seen so far is impressive." Good heavens, Paula thought. I feel like a contestant for Miss America, trying to answer questions in ten seconds flat without offending anyone.

Where was Tom? Oh, yes, standing on the sidelines. Watching. Nodding with approval. Somehow she'd hoped for just a touch of jealousy at the sight of her in another man's arms.

But of course not, Paula realized as Jacques steered her around the edge of the dance floor. She wasn't Tom's wife or even his girl friend; she was his hired companion. Right now she was charming M. d'Armand, and that was exactly what she'd been paid to do.

I'm being unreasonable. Tom's never pretended this was anything but a practical arrangement, she reminded herself, trying to ignore a twinge of pain.

The waltz ended with a flourish. There was another man already at Paula's side requesting the next dance, and she accepted even though she would have preferred to be with Tom. One couldn't afford to be rude to any of the d'Armands' friends.

Her new partner was a red-faced gentleman with an ill-fitting toupee that shifted position as they bounced through a fox-trot. It took all Paula's self-control to keep from giggling.

At last the orchestra concluded with a rendition of "La Marseillaise," and the guests began to disperse.

Several of the men paused to shake hands with Tom on the way out. And Paula was surprised that a number of the women patted her shoulder or arm lightly in farewell, as if they were old friends.

After the others were gone, Simone came over and slid her arm through Paula's. The two women walked slowly toward the stairs together, trailing behind the men.

"You're not used to attending these big affairs with your husband yet, I think, but you have done very well," Simone said. "Much better than I, when I was a bride."

"I could never be as polished as you are." Paula meant every word of it. "The party went perfectly."

Simone gave a small Gallic shrug. "The trick is hiring the right servants. But you will learn for yourself soon. It is not so difficult to give parties when one has nothing else to do."

Again that note of distress. "Surely you do other things as well, especially now that your daughters are older."

"My husband is very traditional." Simone spoke

softly so no one else could hear. "I liked that when I was young—having someone to protect me. But now I think I am a little too much protected."

Then the older woman frowned, as if realizing she'd revealed more than she intended. "But I do not complain, you understand. No one's life can be perfect."

They caught up with the men, and after a flurry of good-nights, Tom and Paula went upstairs.

As soon as the door closed behind them, he caught her close and pressed a lingering kiss onto her lips.

"Mmm." She nestled her head against his shoulder. "Just like an old married couple."

"You're so perfect!" He danced her slowly around the room. "Everybody loved you, and Jacques was impressed. Simone, I gather, is usually very reserved, even with people she knows well, but she took to you right away."

"I wish I had a chance to know her better," Paula said. "And I feel badly, lying to her."

"But it will be worth it." Tom's arms tightened around her. "What a team we make, Paula."

What a team. Yes, it looked like they were going to pull it off, Paula reflected ruefully. Earlier, during their waltz, she'd felt united with him as woman and man. But what he'd seen was a . . . a business consortium.

"Tired?" Tom fluffed his hand through her hair. "I'd say you've earned a bonus. How about a back rub?"

"That sounds great. I'll take a massage anytime."

Paula's muscles were still stiff from the long plane ride, and she deemed it safe enough to let him stroke her. Both of them were too tired to think about romance anyway.

That situation began to change as his fingers unknotted her muscles. Both of them felt it at the same time, the shift in rhythm, the way his hands caressed her shoulders instead of rubbing them, how her breath quickened at his touch.

Someone rapped lightly at the door.

"Drat." Tom went over and opened it a crack. "Yes?"

"Monsieur d'Armand asks if you will join him in his study," said a masculine voice.

"Yes, of course. Just a moment." Tom closed the door and turned back to her resignedly. "Thus ends a promising massage."

Paula sat up. "What do you think he wants?"

Tom ran a comb through his hair and checked his suit in the mirror. "D'Armand's a night owl. Likes to have meetings in the wee hours, or so I've heard. And don't forget he's already checked out my financial situation rather thoroughly. He may be ready to make an offer. Or nix the whole deal."

"Good luck." Paula crossed her fingers.

"If I lose, do I get a consolation prize?" he teased.

"Maybe."

"Gotta go." He crossed the room, kissed her quickly, and left.

Paula lay back nervously. Everything depended on what Jacques d'Armand said in the next few minutes. If he approved the investment, Tom's company would probably make a fortune. If he refused . . .

No doubt Tom would seek the money elsewhere, although she'd gathered that few investors had the amount of capital he needed. But whatever happened, once Jacques and the Jensens were out of the picture, so was she. Because Tom wouldn't need a make-believe wife anymore.

Sometimes, seeing a tender look in his eyes or feeling that—what was the word for it?—kinesthetic sense of where he was even when they weren't looking at each other, she dared to believe she might mean something special to him. But that was foolishness. He was too much like Mickey, viewing everything through a haze of greed. Money was the answer, and "How much?" was the question. Anything else—love, sharing, stability—came in dead last.

Minutes crept by as Paula brushed out her hair, creamed off her makeup, and changed to a nightgown. She hesitated again about sharing his bed, but they'd done it before without problems. It was only a piece of furniture, and considerably more comfortable than the carpet. Paula settled under the covers and closed her eyes.

In spite of her weariness, she found she couldn't sleep until Tom came back and told her what Jacques had said.

She sat up and leafed through a copy of *Newsweek* she'd bought at the airport. After reading the cover story three times without comprehending a word, she gave up.

Footsteps in the hall. The knob turned, and Tom stepped into the room. Expression: determined.

"What happened?" She wrapped her arms around her knees and regarded him expectantly.

"He made me an offer." He pulled off his jacket and hung it in the wardrobe, knocking hangers together with a clatter.

"Is that good?"

"If you consider giving up fifty percent ownership good, it's just terrific." His voice dripped with sarcasm.

"Oh. What did you tell him?"

"I said I'd think about it." He unbuckled his belt. Obviously the fact that she was watching didn't disturb him in the least, so Paula rolled over and looked in the other direction until he finished changing into pajama bottoms.

She told herself she should be grateful the masquerade was apparently over. Perhaps as soon as tomorrow, Mrs. Thomas C. Clinton would cease to exist, except in Paula's wistful memories. "Are we going home right away?"

"Not just yet." He turned off the overhead light and slid into bed beside her. The only illumination came from a lamp on his nightstand, bathing them both in gold.

"We'll be staying here for a while?" Paula curled close, instinctively trying to soothe away his disappointment. "We could tour Paris."

"I promise to take you sight-seeing Monday. We'll give Jacques until then to change his mind." He was watching her speculatively.

Not an amorous look. What was he up to?

"What if he doesn't?" she asked.

"We're going to the Riviera for a few days. Jacques has generously offered to lend us his villa at Cap-Ferrat for the rest of our belated honeymoon."

Paula didn't like the sound of this. "Why do I get the feeling there's something you're not telling me?"

Tom chuckled. "You don't miss a trick, Paula. You're the perfect companion for a scam like this."

"Hey!" She sat up, unaware of how the soft light played across her silky gown and the inviting curves of her body. "You said we weren't up to anything unethical."

"We're not . . . exactly." He laced his fingers behind his head and pursed his lips as he studied her. "I don't suppose I could persuade you to sleep in the nude? Not that you don't look enticing with a little lace on, but we might think of something to do in the middle of the night."

Paula folded her arms in front of her protectively. "It is the middle of the night," she snapped, her good mood evaporating. "I want to know what scheme you've cooked up this time, Tom Clinton."

"I merely hinted to our host that he wasn't the only man in France interested in Clinton Computers," Tom said.

"Oh?"

"I happen to know some bankers on the Riviera who might be willing to make a deal. For considerably less than fifty percent." He was wearing that gambler's expression again, eager for the next roll of the dice.

"You don't really know any bankers, do you?"

"As a matter of fact, I do," Tom said. "One of them was here tonight, and he extended an invitation to have lunch if we should happen to be going to Nice. He's heading down that way himself."

Paula frowned. Something about this didn't ring true. "But you mentioned a scam."

"I do know some bankers, and they do have enough money, but it's highly unlikely they'd be interested in anything as speculative as what I have in mind," Tom explained. "I'm hoping Jacques isn't as sure of that as I am."

"Oh, no." Paula slid under the covers again. "I'm supposed to keep up this pretense for yet another bunch of people? We won't get away with it, and my reputation will be ruined."

Tom started to laugh. The deep resonance filled

the room and shook the bed.

"What's so funny?"

It took a moment before he could speak. "Do you think... do you think the opinion of a bunch of French financiers...is going to make any difference—"

"To an Anaheim cleaning lady? Thanks. I know I'm not in your class, Tom, but you don't have to rub it in." She rolled away from him, her pride smarting furiously.

"Hey, I didn't mean it that way." His lips grazed the nape of her neck. "But this is Fantasyland, Paula. You'll never have to see these people again."

That's right, she thought dully. After this caper ended, she wouldn't be a part of Tom Clinton's life. Except to clean his apartment on Fridays. What would Simone d'Armand think if she knew about that?

"I've had enough," she said, scrunching up her neck to discourage his tickling kisses. "If you want to go to the Riviera, you'll have to go without me."

"You're tired." Tom reached over and turned out the light. "We'll talk about this in the morning."

Paula lay there stiffly until she heard his breathing become regular.

No matter how persuasive Tom might be, she didn't dare go with him to the Riviera. Her feelings tonight showed that she'd almost reached the point of no return. Any longer sharing a room with him and she'd probably find herself slipping over the edge.

Paula had spent too long picking up the pieces after her divorce from Mickey to let herself in for that again. No, she'd better go home while her heart remained in one piece.

A little chipped, maybe. But still whole.

CHAPTER *Six*

THE NEXT DAY was Sunday and, despite their weariness, Paula and Tom arose early to go to church with the d'Armands. The service, in French, was conducted at a village church near the estate rather than in a large cathedral as Paula had expected.

Simone's eyes looked red beneath her small-brimmed hat. Simple exhaustion, or had she and Jacques had an argument? Her husband was as courteously correct as ever, but Paula thought she detected a harsh set to his jaw that hadn't been there the previous evening.

After they returned home, Tom accepted an invitation from Simone for a tennis match. Paula lingered on the terrace beside Jacques, both of them sipping coffee as sunlight filtered through a vine-covered trellis.

Her host drummed his fingers on the arm of the chair, his gaze fixed on the two distant figures dashing about the tennis court.

"Do you play?" Paula asked.

"What?" He swung around, startled.

"Tennis. Do you play tennis?" It had seemed a safe enough topic, but she was beginning to wonder.

"No, I'm a horseman, like my daughter." He paused. "Are you a sportswoman, Madame Clinton?"

"Who, me? It's as much as I can do to push a vacuum cleaner around all day." Realizing what she'd said, she caught her breath.

But Jacques regarded her approvingly. "You aren't too proud to do your own housework. It's good that a woman takes such care with her home."

"I think family life is very important," Paula agreed, releasing her breath. He didn't suspect anything.

"You don't want a career?" he probed. "I understand with many American women, that is what comes first."

"I like things the way they are." She'd rather not lie any more baldly than necessary.

"Good, very good," he said. "It's unfortunate that many older women see a glamorous image of what life is like for girls today and they become dissatisfied."

Now, she realized, he was talking about Simone. So they had indeed had a disagreement. "People do change." Paula watched Simone slam the ball into Tom's court. "Sometimes what suits a woman—or a man—at one stage of their life isn't the best thing at another time."

She'd meant to help Simone, but instead Jacques took her comment another way. "That is exactly my viewpoint," he said. "My wife wants to return to her younger days, when she was an actress. A friend of hers, a crazy Greek woman, performs with a theater company in Nice. She has asked Simone to come and work with them for a few months. But it is not suitable—as you say, at this stage of her life. She is not an unmarried girl anymore."

The tennis game ended prematurely, and the two players returned. "Simone has a headache," Tom explained as their hostess went up to her room.

No wonder, Paula thought.

She and Tom also retreated. She decided against relating her conversation with Jacques. Tom would probably disapprove of her meddling.

The two of them spent the day relaxing, napping and swimming in the outdoor pool. With Jacques apt to pass by at any time, they kept their behavior strictly proper, much to Paula's relief.

As soon as she got her tour of Paris, she was going home, she told herself, wondering why Tom made no further mention of the trip to the Riviera. If he believed she would change her mind, he was sadly mistaken.

Simone remained closeted for the rest of the day, and Jacques said little at meals. No mention was made of the loan, but from time to time one of the men would regard the other thoughtfully. Paula had a mental image of two cats circling each other.

She and Tom played two-handed poker that night, neither of them concentrating much. Paula, still suffering from jet lag, nodded off with three aces in her hand.

On Monday, Tom woke her up at eight A.M. Rising to consciousness through a fog of sleep, Paula muttered, "Go stick your tail in a light socket."

"You certainly are grumpy in the morning." He sat on the edge of the bed, already dressed. "I'd have let you nap a while longer, but the car will be here in half an hour."

"The car?"

"For our tour of Paris."

The reminder galvanized her into action: She leaped out of bed and into the shower. Within half an hour, her hunger assuaged by a cup of coffee from a silver tray, Paula was ready for action in tan slacks, an off-white blouse, and a suede jacket. She tucked a camera into her pocket for good measure. It might be years before she had another chance to visit Paris, and she intended to make the most of it.

The car came complete with chauffeur. "Monsieur d'Armand is certainly generous," she observed as Tom helped her into the rear seat.

"As a host, anyway." He said no more, and she suspected he didn't want the chauffeur to repeat any derogatory remarks to d'Armand.

The driver turned out to be an excellent guide, commenting in English as they drove down the broad Champs-Élysées with its grand cinemas and elegant shops. They circled the Arc de Triomphe, which rose incongruously amid legions of honking automobiles.

The chauffeur made a stop at the Eiffel Tower, even volunteering to take a photograph of Paula and Tom together beneath the thousand-foot-high lacy tower. And he added a bit of knowledge to Paula's store: The same Alexandre Gustave Eiffel who designed the tower had engineered the Statue of Liberty.

Next they took a whirl around Montmartre, the bohemian village with its steep stone steps, open terraces, and sidewalk cafés. Artists sat at easels, painting the scene and offering their works for sale.

"Let's walk around," Paula urged.

"This is for tourists," Tom said. "Wait until we get to the Left Bank. That's where the real French people go."

"Are there artists?" she asked.

"But of course." He faked a French accent, rather charmingly, she thought.

They decided to make good use of the car that morning and give the driver the afternoon off. So, for the next few hours, they sped through the highlights of Paris.

The things Paula remembered best were the Bois de Boulogne's spectacular gardens, the opera house, and the Louvre.

Inside the museum, they stopped to admire the Mona Lisa and the Venus de Milo. But when Paula wandered toward the Egyptian antiquities, Tom tugged her firmly back to the car.

"We could spend a week in here," he told her. "And we've only got one day for the whole city."

By midafternoon she was more than happy to sink into a chair at a café on the Left Bank's Boulevard St-Michel. They enjoyed a cup of espresso and a ham-and-cheese sandwich.

People swirled past them, stylishly dressed women in high heels, students in torn jeans, tourists festooned with cameras.

"I'd like to spend a few weeks here," Paula said. "We passed some stunning shops, although they're probably out of my price range. Isn't it a law that tourists have to buy at least one bottle of perfume when they visit France?"

"No doubt." Tom was watching her with the same expression he'd worn all day, the delighted look of a child showing off his toys. "I don't think I've ever enjoyed Paris as much as I have today, introducing it to you."

Paula gazed up in surprise. His tan eyes caught her

blue ones and held them for a tender moment.

Something funny was happening to her heart. It seemed to be under the impression it had entered a tango contest.

"I . . . I never thought I'd actually get here." Paula lowered her eyelashes in sudden shyness. "I almost can't believe it, even now. Going home will be such a letdown."

"Then postpone it," he urged. "Come to the Riviera. I'll take you to Monte Carlo, wherever you want. If you pass this up, you'll always regret it."

Paula set her jaw firmly. "But I might be even sorrier if I go. No dice, Tom."

"Can't blame a fellow for trying."

After they finished eating, they began the promised stroll down the boulevard. Her arm linked with Tom's, Paula felt like a youngster at the circus.

There were antique shops, dress boutiques, record stores, and *pâtisseries* with artfully contrived fruit tarts displayed in their windows. The two of them popped inside one bakeshop to purchase a half dozen of the treats before moving on, sticky-fingered.

The avenue ended at the Seine, and they turned to walk beside it. The vast cathedral of Notre-Dame soared ahead of them while, along the sidewalk, artists and bookstalls attracted knots of browsers.

"When I come here, I feel as if I've stepped into another world." Tom paused to take in the panorama. "A slower, gentler time full of enchanted lovers."

This was a side of Tom that Paula had never seen before, poetic and contemplative. She rested her cheek against his shoulder.

A group of students, dressed like Americans in blue jeans and T-shirts yet somehow managing to look thoroughly French, laughed and elbowed each other good-naturedly as they crossed the street nearby.

"I wish I could have come here when I was young." Tom and Paula resumed their walk along the river. "There's a lightness of spirit that I feel here. . . . I missed all that when I was in college."

"Why?" Paula asked. The campus of the junior college she'd attended couldn't compare with Paris, but she'd had some good times with her friends.

"When I wasn't studying, I was working." Tom's eyes had a sad, faraway look. "I was a short-order cook in the evening, believe it or not, and an auto-jockey at the car wash on weekends."

"Two jobs?" Paula tightened her grip on his arm, sympathetically. "Couldn't you get a scholarship?"

"I had one." They had moved close enough to Notre-Dame to make out the gargoyles poised overhead like creatures from a horror film. "Most of the money went to my family. We . . . had a lot of medical bills."

Paula remembered the photograph in the apartment. "Was it your sister?" she asked. "The girl in the wheelchair?"

He glanced down at her, startled. "How did you—oh, I ought to remember that cleaning ladies see everything."

Paula waited as the silence between them lengthened, hoping he'd say more, pretending meanwhile to be absorbed by a stall selling French comic books.

"Yes, that was my sister," Tom said finally, his voice tight with emotion. "She died when I was fifteen. Now how did we get onto such a gloomy subject? This is supposed to be our day to have fun."

He switched to a description of the history of Notre-Dame, and in spite of her curiosity Paula soon became absorbed in the beauty of the stained glass windows and the awesome grandeur of the great structure.

Her legs ached from walking by the time the chauffeur returned to whisk them back to the d'Armand estate for a predinner nap. Paula protested, certain that she wouldn't sleep a wink, but in fact she sank into unconsciousness for several hours.

Their host and hostess had already left for the evening by the time she awoke, the butler informed them. Paula wasn't entirely sorry to have Tom to herself on what was likely to be their last night together.

Refreshed and clad in her favorite aquamarine evening dress, she descended from the car into the cool air of a Parisian evening. Rue Gustave-Flaubert was an elegant street, and Tom's anticipatory gleam told her the restaurant he'd selected was a favorite.

She could see why as soon as they entered, their footsteps hushed by the maroon carpets. The atmosphere was one of subdued luxury: brown colors accented by burnt orange, lace curtains draping the arched windows, and fresh flowers set at each table.

The maître d' ushered them quickly to a private table in an alcove, presenting Tom with a wine list before departing.

"It's lovely," Paula said, gazing with interest at the other diners. "What an intimate atmosphere."

"I'm glad you noticed." Tom looked up from the wine list with a warm smile.

The meal was sumptuous: duck liver in brioche, a delicious seafood dish called *coquilles St-Jacques,* and an array of desserts that would have set Weight Watchers back ten years.

"Do you come here often?" Paula asked, taking a last sip of the excellent wine Tom had selected.

"Whenever I get the chance." He leaned back and regarded her.

"I guess I don't really know very much about you," Paula said. "You seem to have enjoyed your millions while you had them, at any rate."

"Too much so." Tom made a tent of his fingers on the tablecloth. "I went a little crazy when I first started to make money— traveling, buying cars, doing the things I'd always dreamed of. Somehow I thought there would always be plenty of money for the things that really mattered."

"Such as what?" Paula asked.

"Oh, I have my pet projects," he said evasively. Then his tone softened as he leaned forward. "And speaking of pet projects, you're definitely one of them."

His eyes caressed her face. Today, after spending these hours in each other's company, she sensed that he, too, felt the special magic between them. For this suspended moment, they ceased to be employer and employee, millionaire and cleaning lady, and became the essence of man and woman.

His fingers touched the back of her hand across the table with a jolt of electricity. Suddenly the room that had seemed enticingly intimate became far, far too public.

"Shall we go?" he said, and she nodded.

They rode back to the estate in silence, her mind hovering loosely somewhere above her head, more as a result of Tom's nearness than of the half-bottle of wine she'd consumed.

There was no sign of Jacques or Simone when they arrived. Tom caught Paula's hand as she started toward the elevator. "Let's not go up yet. I'd like to take a walk in the garden."

Her mood still euphoric, she accompanied him through the house to a rear door that opened on wonderland.

Here everything was freshness, the night air scented with roses. A white gravel path led between banks of flowering shrubs, and the moon gazed down at them benignly.

"Three-quarter moon," Tom noted. "Courtesy of our host, no doubt."

Paula giggled. "Does he control everything in France?"

"Everything but me."

"And me!" She swung around, holding onto Tom's hands. "I wish we had our own private orchestra. We could dance out here, by ourselves."

"Your wish is my command, madame. The Clinton choir, at your service." Tom bowed low and then began to hum "The Blue Danube" waltz.

His clear baritone caught the rhythm, three-quarter time beneath a three-quarter moon, and Paula joined in. He laid one hand on her waist, and they danced across the gravel, humming together.

Tom segued into another waltz, and then another. In the heady sensation of spinning about the garden, Paula felt herself in another world. A world inhabited exclusively by the two of them, now and forever.

His grip tightened on her waist, and she felt the heat of his body through the delicate fabric of her dress.

"Do you believe in reincarnation?" Tom murmured, navigating expertly around a rosebush.

"I don't know," she said. "Do you?"

"I think we've been here before." His grave tone raised prickles along her spine. "We must have been lovers long ago. Perhaps we died in each other's arms."

"What an eerie thought." Suddenly the garden filled with ghosts, men and women in powdered wigs and embroidered costumes, tracing minuets to unheard music.

"I'm sorry." Tom stopped. "I've spoiled our mood, haven't I? For some reason I just felt very sad. Do you really have to go home tomorrow, Paula? I wish you'd stay."

She trembled and let him pull her close. Her head rested against the silky security of his coat. "I'd like to stay here forever," she confessed, "but I can't. You wouldn't understand."

"No?" He lifted her chin. "You're impulsive, but when it comes to taking a planned risk, you frighten easily, don't you?"

She'd never thought of it that way. Paula knew she wasn't timid, and yet the possibility of staying with Tom in a secluded Riviera villa filled her with apprehension.

"Suppose it isn't a planned risk but a sure failure?" She met his gaze squarely. "I'm not an eighteen-year-old kid fresh out of school. I don't think the whole world is going to fall into my lap just because I want it to."

"You don't need the whole world; just a little piece of the sky." His lips teased against her ear. "With one or two stars in it. Maybe even a comet, if we're lucky."

"Comets burn out." Her hands clenched with the effort of resisting.

"Everything dies eventually." His hands feathered up her back. "Life is a temporary condition."

"Oh, Tom." She pulled away. "It sounds wonderful, this talk about ghosts and stars and risks. But I'm the cleaning lady, remember? I know about the champagne bottles lying around on the floor the morning after, and ashes growing stale in the fireplace, and the crumpled clothes that have to be picked off the floor and laundered."

"And that's your view of life?" He shook his head in disbelief. "Come on, Paula, I know you better than that. It's my own fault for talking about death and the past. Let's dance some more."

"All right," she agreed reluctantly. If she'd had a room to herself, she would have retreated, but the idea of accompanying Tom to their shared bedroom was too intimidating to deal with.

He hummed "Some Enchanted Evening," and they sang the words together. "Younger Than Springtime" followed naturally, and then other Rodgers and Hammerstein tunes.

By the time they'd run out of songs and Tom had guided her back toward the house, Paula's good mood was restored.

"I never felt truly at ease with a woman until I met you," Tom observed when the door to their room had shut behind them and they stood in the warm lamp glow. "Imagine me, humming songs to dance by."

"My turn." Paula launched into a slightly off-key rendition of "I Could Have Danced All Night." With a flourish, Tom guided her around the room.

It was different, holding each other close in this small space. There was no moon to watch over them like a third presence, no evening breeze to dissipate the warmth of their bodies, no sense that they might be intruded upon.

Their pace slowed, and the dance grew more languid. The only accompaniment was the rapid beating of their hearts and the memory of a waltz.

"It's amazing how our bodies fit together." Tom cupped her derriere lightly, pulling her closer against him until it felt as if their bodies would merge.

"This could be fatal," Paula murmured.

"I like to play with fire." His tongue found the shell of her ear, tantalizing toward the core and then withdrawing at the last moment.

"You tease," she accused softly.

By way of an answer, his head lowered to hers and his tongue traced the contours of her lips. Her mouth parted to welcome him, but he delayed, licking lightly across the inner edge of her lips.

Paula stood on tiptoe and pulled him closer until at last his tongue penetrated her teeth, into the molten interior. Their bodies stretched length to length, her nipples responding to his hard chest and his masculinity swelling at the nearness of her body.

"Oh, Tom," she whispered, drawing her head back by inches but unable to make any further move. "We mustn't do this."

"Why not?" His eyes gleamed with desire. "Don't torture us both this way. Lying beside you last night—you thought I was asleep, didn't you?—I nearly went crazy. I need you, Paula."

Need, love. Maybe they were the same thing. She knew now that what she'd felt for Mickey had been more a longing for security than real love. But she'd never felt this passion, this hunger within, that Tom aroused.

"It won't change," she whispered. "I'll still go home in the morning."

"Will you?" His thumbs ran down the sides of her

neck and along her thin gold necklace. He stroked the pearl pendant, his faint pressure on the chain holding her prisoner.

"I have to, Tom." Her throat clamped dryly over the words, but she forced them out.

"Do you?" He slid open the clasp and lifted away the necklace. Her throat felt naked and vulnerable.

"If we make love, nothing can come of it. It's only passion, it won't last."

"I'll take my chances." His tongue brushed the hollow of her collarbone, flicking out to moisten the pulsing curve. His mouth searched lower, toward the deeply rounded neckline of her gown.

"Tom..."

In a last spurt of determination, she tried to pull away but lost her balance and fell against him. He stumbled, and with a startled cry the two of them toppled to the floor.

Paula lay motionless for a moment, the wind knocked out of her. In the fall, her dress had hiked up to reveal slender thighs, a fact that Tom didn't miss from where he'd landed beside her.

How delightful and dangerous he looked, with his hair rumpled and his eyes alight. Like a pirate who'd just opened the lid of a treasure chest.

"You tell me when you want me to stop." He ran his hand the length of her leg, from the narrow ankle to the bared hip. "Now?"

She didn't answer. The effort that knocked them to the floor had depleted her resistance.

He followed the insides of her calves, knees, thighs, and proceeded up her body. One hand reached behind and unzipped the dress, pulling it off to disclose the delicate lace beneath.

She ought to push him away. She ought to rise and put on her bathrobe. She didn't move.

"Soft," he murmured. His thumbs followed the perimeter of the lace across the top of her breasts, and then he lowered the slip straps, loosely trapping her arms as he bared her breasts to his gaze.

Paula closed her eyes for the assault and instead felt his breath whisper across her nipples.

"Had enough?" His voice was low, provoking. She let the question die in the silent air.

His teeth nipped gently at the tips of her breasts, drawing a moan from deep within her. Tom pulled away the slip and bra, and with her wordless cooperation stripped off the pantyhose, leaving only a minuscule bit of cloth to hide the last secrets of her body.

"Want me to quit?" The heels of his hands pressed over her breasts with a hint of roughness, sending hot desire flooding through her.

By way of response, Paula reached for his shirt and unbuttoned it. Tom shrugged away the restraining garment, displaying the curling expanse of hair across his broad chest and muscular shoulders.

Then, as if impatient with delays, he threw off the rest of his clothing and removed her panties.

They were naked together, but not touching. Paula lay on the carpet gazing up at Tom from between her lashes, admiring the masculine richness of him, aching to feel his roughness against her satiny skin.

Tom studied her, his mouth curving upward with satisfaction. "Now," he teased, "don't forget to tell me when to quit."

He crouched over her, keeping their bodies apart as his lips brushed hers.

Slowly, tauntingly, he explored her. Silver sensations penetrated her breasts and stomach, her hips and thighs. And she wanted more. She wanted him to take everything.

Paula pulled him down over her, her tongue penetrating his mouth. The movement unleashed his caged passion, and he returned urgency with urgency.

He was over her, around her, holding and mastering her. Inside her, with powerful thrusts that filled and emptied her. Paula caught at his shoulders as if she were drowning.

His flesh rubbed against hers, coarse and wild. He pinned her wrists to the floor and slowed his assault, barely restraining the fierce hunger they shared.

She moved to his rhythm, tempting and inflaming him. He poised overhead and then, with hard swift demands, plunged them both into a vortex of fire and longing.

Heat and flame, flame and heat. Paula twisted, clutched him, wanting more and more. Then it came, the explosion that glittered through her body, scattering sparks across her skin and leaving her breathless in a warm glow.

Tom lay beside her, his arms cradling her, his breathing rapid and irregular. They were both drenched with sweat.

"Paula"—he kissed her lazily—"should I stop now?"

She laughed.

CHAPTER

Seven

PAULA AWOKE TO the sound of the shower running in the bathroom. She lifted her head, saw that it was a mere seven o'clock, and decided to get up anyway.

She padded across the floor and stood in the doorway, gazing at the rippled glass door that transformed Tom's body into an impressionist work of art. Then she slid it open and stepped into the hot spray. His wet skin gleamed, and she rubbed against him with catlike pleasure.

"Is there someone in here with me?" Tom queried from beneath a mound of shampoo bubbles. As if there could be any doubt! "Hello?" He groped around in pretended blindness, his hands finding their way over Paula's spray-slicked curves.

She cuddled against him, waiting until he rinsed away the soap and blinked down at her.

"Well, my goodness," said Tom. "It's the cleaning lady."

"You look clean enough to me," she shot back. "My turn." And she ducked her hair under the shower before applying shampoo.

They emerged a few minutes later, feeling warm

and close. Tom lifted down their suitcases from atop one of the wardrobes.

"What time do I have to be at the airport?" Paula asked, lowering her slip over her head.

"The train leaves around eleven-thirty."

She pulled the slip into place and regarded him suspiciously. "What train?"

"The one to the Riviera."

Paula debated briefly whether to argue and decided against it. Now that she and Tom were lovers, there was no point in giving up the chance to spend a few more days together.

She began folding underwear into her valise.

It was difficult not to be distracted as Tom, unabashedly nude, stood hanging his suits in his garment bag. It was also difficult to believe they'd become this intimate, and that in less than a week it was going to end.

He never told me he loved me, she reflected as she applied makeup and then packed her cosmetic case. But what difference would it have made anyway if he said it in the heat of passion? Men would say anything to get what they wanted from a woman.

Mickey had taught her about promises. He made lots of them: not to gamble, not to flirt with other women, not to fight with his boss again, not to get fired. He meant every one of them, too, at least for the thirty seconds it took to utter them.

She'd avoided entanglements with men since her divorce, and she'd never expected to let herself go this far with Tom. But now that she had, Paula saw no sense in deluding herself about the future.

They finished packing and headed downstairs together.

The French don't make a big meal of breakfast the way Americans do. This morning Paula and Tom descended to a repast of coffee and buttery fresh croissants. Not a slice of bacon or an egg in sight.

Simone joined them to say good-bye, sunglasses not quite covering the dark circles under her eyes. As she was about to sit down, Jacques walked in. After a moment's hesitation, Simone excused herself and left the room.

"I hope you enjoy Cap-Ferrat," Jacques told them, ignoring his wife's departure. "The housekeeper has been advised that you're coming."

"We really appreciate your generosity," Paula said. How strange it felt to stand here making polite chitchat when it was obvious that something was wrong. Paula's heart went out to Simone; wished there was something she could do to help.

The two men shook hands, their eyes meeting momentarily. The game wasn't over, on either side.

The d'Armands' chauffeur drove them to the train station where, with fluent French, Tom navigated their way through a maze of ticket agents and harried travelers.

"Are you sure this is the right train?" Paula asked as they settled into a luxurious compartment that might have come from a James Bond movie set. "The sign on one of the cars said Barcelona."

"That's the trick to European trains." Tom stowed their luggage in the rack overhead. "You have to make sure you're in the right car. The train splits up. Some of the cars will indeed go to Barcelona, but not this one."

Paula thought it might have been nice to get on the wrong train and spend a week or so wandering around

Spain. Or Italy. Or almost anywhere, as long as she and Tom were together.

The train wasn't crowded, and they had the compartment to themselves, something Tom assured her would be impossible a week later. Everyone in Paris went on vacation in August, and the trains would be crammed.

Paula watched in delight as the verdant French countryside rolled past, with an occasional castle visible in the distance. At one of the stops, Tom bought sandwiches and soft drinks through the window from a station vendor.

It was evening by the time they arrived in Nice. Here the bustle and confusion seemed almost as great as in Paris, and she was grateful for Tom's skill in unloading them and locating the rental car.

"Where are the nude beaches?" Paula asked as the Renault coursed through a square rimmed by colonnaded walkways and shops.

"Have you no sense of history?" Tom demanded. "Don't you want to see the traces of Roman settlements, the artworks by Picasso . . ."

"Is this where you got the print?"

That stopped him for about five seconds. "Oh. The Picasso in the apartment. Yes, as a matter of fact. In my wilder days."

Paula giggled. "Arthur Jensen would have been offended, if it hadn't been a gift from Aunt What's-her-name."

Tom grinned and rested one arm across the seat, just touching the back of her neck.

They headed west, past seclusion walls draped with flowering vines. Tom consulted a map several times with a flashlight, turned down a winding lane, and finally entered a private drive. It led to a low, rambling home built of white stucco.

"Voilà," he said.

They'd barely exited the car before the front door opened and a buxom middle-aged woman hurried out. *"Bonsoir! Bonsoir!"* she cried, waving her hands in greeting. *"Monsieur et Madame Clinton! Bienvenu!"*

As the woman welcomed them, Paula gathered that she was Marie, the housekeeper, and that she'd begun to worry when they hadn't arrived sooner. Fortunately, she spoke reasonably good English.

A meal had been prepared of a regional specialty, *salade Niçoise*—or Nice salad—complete with anchovies and olives, along with an omelet and, for dessert, *crème caramel.*

They ate companionably. The house, in contrast to the formal decor of the Paris estate, had been designed with a casual air. The dining room flowed into the living room, and a wealth of plants accentuated the natural feeling of the architecture.

Afterward, while Paula unpacked, Tom made phone calls. He rejoined her later, looking pleased with himself.

"Well?" she said. "Care to confide in a fellow conspirator?"

"Perhaps." Tom strode over and took Paula in his arms. "I've hardly kissed you all day." He made up for the lack, at length.

"Let me help you out of those hot clothes," she murmured, and unbuttoned his shirt.

They stripped each other, garment by garment. A cool breeze blew over them through partly opened French windows.

Tom rolled Paula on top of him and kissed her

again, both of them moving with languid sensuality.

The pace of their union intensified. He pulled her tight against him and claimed her with an urgency that demanded total acquiescence, total acceptance. Paula took him into herself and shuddered with the delight of it, riding a river of joy into an ocean of pleasure.

Afterward, he said, "About tomorrow."

"Hmmm?"

"I was going to tell you about tomorrow."

She nestled her head in the hollow of his shoulder. "What about it?"

"My contacts seem to be paying off." His voice resonated through his body; she felt rather than heard it. "I'm having lunch with a banker—this one's solo, so you'll have a chance to sunbathe—and we're invited to a party tomorrow night."

"That was quick work," she murmured sleepily. "Do you think Jacques will hear about it?"

Tom chuckled. "I can tell you one thing. He didn't lend us his villa out of pure nobility."

"What do you mean?"

"He's keeping his eye on us." Tom pulled the covers over her. "I expect we'll be seeing him again."

The next morning was the first time Paula had been alone since she and Tom became lovers. Being with him constantly felt quite natural, she reflected as she gave herself an informal tour of the house. Marie and a young assistant had a talent for staying inconspicuous, and Paula felt free to wander through the rambling rooms and grounds.

Perhaps she and Tom could stay friends after they returned home. But I have to be realistic about this, she told herself sternly as she sipped a cup of coffee in the sun-washed breakfast room.

The two of them lived in different worlds. His was full of wealthy, sophisticated people who played for high stakes. Paula could fit in with them when she tried, but she knew that at heart she didn't belong there. Pretending was fine, for an evening or a week, but not for a lifetime.

And she wasn't so sure Tom would fit into her world either, the world she planned for herself.

There was no room in it for gamblers, for bluffers and card sharks. She'd vowed when she divorced Mickey that never again would she give herself to a man only to be left empty-handed, with the years passing by and her dreams of a secure family becoming less and less attainable.

I'd better enjoy this while it lasts and then move on before I get trapped, she decided, finishing her coffee and returning to their room. A man like Tom could keep her dangling for years, living on dreams and hope. If she weren't careful.

Paula removed her slacks and blouse and donned a crocheted pink bikini. She hesitated before the mirror, wondering if Marie would be shocked.

It certainly didn't leave much to the imagination. Paula's sleekly tanned shoulders, nipped-in waist, and long legs were completely exposed. Only the bare essentials were covered, and the crocheting gave the impression one might get a glimpse of the rest at any moment.

She'd bought the swimsuit in a little boutique on Balboa Island back home, and packed it on impulse. It hardly took up any space.

Well, this is the Riviera, she reminded herself.

Everyone will probably think I'm conservative, wearing anything at all.

She went out through the French windows, following a path of artfully placed flat stones to the swimming pool.

The area around it was landscaped for privacy, with clumps of ferns and iris, making it harder than she'd expected to find a patch of sun. Paula shifted the chaise longue until she got the angle right, then stretched out on her back.

She dozed off listening to the idle twitter of birds and wondering what sorts of feathered creatures inhabited these parts. If she were rich, perhaps she'd take up bird-watching...

A shadow fell across her, and the sudden coolness woke Paula.

Her eyes blinked open, and she found herself looking into the equally startled face of Simone d'Armand.

"Hi." Tom had said Jacques was keeping an eye on them, but Paula hadn't expected their hosts this soon. "What a pleasant surprise."

"Yes," Simone answered, sitting in one of the canvas chairs. She was more casually dressed than at the estate, wearing designer jeans and a silk blouse that emphasized her pencil slimness. "I didn't realize you were staying here."

"You didn't?" Paula sat up and hugged her knees to keep her balance. "I assumed Jacques had told you. Where is he?"

"Still in Paris, I believe." Simone shaded her eyes against the sunlight. "He should be here in a few days."

Why hadn't he mentioned that his wife would be joining them? Paula wondered. And why hadn't he told Simone he'd invited the Clintons to stay here?

"Well, I'm glad we'll have a chance to get to know each other better," Paula said. "Will you be staying for a while?"

"No. . . . not exactly." Simone stared across the pool for a moment, lost in thought, before continuing. "My friend Melina has invited me to stay at her house in St-Paul-de-Vence; it's not far from here."

That must be the actress who wanted Simone to join her theater group in Nice, Paula realized. "But this is your house. I don't want to drive you away."

"Not at all." Simone smiled, the first sign of relaxation she'd shown that morning. "I only came by to pick up some of my summer clothes. Melina isn't expecting me this early, so I came out here to get some sun."

"I see." Paula wondered how to bring up the question that was troubling her: whether Simone had left her husband. "Are you and Jacques taking seperate vacations?"

"Yes, yes," Simone said a touch too quickly. "That's right. I wanted a chance to visit Melina. And that gives me an idea. There is a party tonight; perhaps you and Tom could come."

"I think we already have an engagement." Paula felt sure Simone's party would be much more fun. "Some banker he knows invited us."

"Oh, perhaps it is the same one," Simone said. "We are more casual here in the South. The financiers and the film and theater people often mix. Let us hope to see each other tonight, then."

She stood up, gesturing to Paula to remain seated. "*A bientôt.*"

That meant "see you soon," Paula remembered as

she watched Simone's trim figure disappear into the house.

Why couldn't Jacques be more flexible, more accepting of his wife as an individual? Paula wondered sadly. Despite the couple's estrangement, she sensed the commitment and love it had taken to raise two daughters together and share a home over the years. Did Jacques really see Simone only as a beautiful ornament? Surely they must have weathered some storms together and he must have glimpsed the intelligent, unique woman beneath the manicured exterior.

If only there were something she could do besides nodding politely and pretending to believe Simone was just on vacation. But what?

Restless, Paula gave up on the sunbath and returned to the bedroom. She came in the French windows at the same time Tom was entering through the door.

"What a vision!" He stood there taking in her bikini-clad form, his lips pursed in admiration. "And you smell wonderful. Sun brings out a musk scent I can't resist."

Tom crossed the room and caught Paula about the waist, pulling her against his ivory silk jacket. After a brief kiss, she stepped away.

"You just missed a visit from Simone," she said.

"Simone d'Armand?"

"Yes, she's . . . visiting a friend nearby." Paula hesitated, not wanting to reveal too much of what, after all, was Simone's private affair. "I think she and Jacques are having some problems."

"And in your disguise as Wonder Woman you're planning to swoop down and miraculously solve everything?" he teased.

She had to laugh at the image of herself flying

through the air in a star-spangled Wonder Woman costume. "I wish I could."

"You're a soft touch, sweetheart—as I ought to know." He caught her hips and drew her close, his mouth relentlessly finding hers.

Paula yielded, flinging her arms around him and kissing him passionately. She'd missed him that day more than she realized.

"Wow!" Tom pulled her down beside him on the edge of the bed. "Let's see what you're hiding under that knitted Band-Aid."

"Crocheted Band-Aid," Paula teased. "Well, let's see." She lowered one strap and glanced at the mark left underneath. "Looks like a white line."

"And a matching one over here." Tom lowered her other strap. "You should try tanning in the nude."

Paula reached behind her to untie the bikini top. The knot was stuck. She tugged at it futilely.

"Need some help?" Tom turned her so he could reach the knot. "This thing really is tight. I think I need a wrench."

"Just as long as you don't use scissors," she replied.

He battled with the thing for several minutes. "No luck. Can you pull it off over your head?"

She wriggled, and he worked the wisp of material gradually upward. It stuck around her shoulders, pinning her arms above her head, and Tom paused to enjoy the sight of her bare breasts.

Paula felt the nipples tighten beneath his gaze. "I think I like you this way," Tom said.

"Get this thing off." She struggled some more, but her movements only served to tighten the knot.

"We'd better check and see if the other knots are jammed." Tom tugged the strings that held her bikini bottom together at the hip. The panties fell away from her.

Paula frowned, her arms locked over her head. "Maybe you should put some oil on it. That might help."

"Good idea." Tom rummaged in the bathroom cabinet for a moment and returned with a bottle of scented oil. Instead of applying it to the knot, however, he smoothed it over Paula's breasts, stomach, and thighs.

"What do you think you're doing?"

"Having a wonderful time."

Paula squirmed half-heartedly as he ran his hands up and down her slick body. She was beginning to enjoy the situation. She only hoped she wasn't going to be stranded in this embarrassing position forever.

"You might be more comfortable if you lay down," Tom observed and, spreading a towel to protect the bedspread, pushed her gently onto her back.

He drew off his clothes and lay beside her, rubbing his body against hers until they were both covered with oil.

"You wait until I get my hands on you, Tom Clinton!" she joked.

"I can think of lots of delicious things you could do with those hands, but it'll have to wait for another time." Tom shook his head in mock despair. "We may have to call in the locksmith. Wait till he gets a look at this."

Paula giggled, then gasped as his tongue rasped across her breasts. "That oil doesn't taste bad," he observed, his thumbs circling the insides of her thighs. His mouth moved lower, and Paula shuddered with ecstasy.

"Oh, Tom," she whispered.

He joined them together smoothly, their bodies glistening against each other, flesh sliding over flesh with a silky sensation of pure sensuality.

They floated in scented oil, hot and exotic, as their passion mounted. Tom's movements became harder, and Paula matched them thrust for thrust until a wave of fire engulfed them both.

As they lay side by side, spent and happy, Paula realized the oil-soaked bikini knot had finally begun to work its way loose.

CHAPTER *Eight*

AS SHE WAS dressing that evening, Paula remembered what Simone had said about the party and told Tom. "Do you suppose it's the same one?" she asked.

"I certainly hope so." He grinned. "What better way to get word to Jacques about how well my deal is progressing? There'll be some important people there, and I don't mind being seen with them."

"I don't like using people, especially someone I consider a friend." Paula slipped a pair of artfully constructed fake sapphire earrings into place.

"Simone d'Armand?" Tom whistled as he knotted his tie in front of the mirror. "Don't get carried away, Paula. She's a charming lady, but she knows how to keep people at a distance. Don't assume you mean any more to her than a business opportunity for her husband."

Paula doubted very much that Simone was worried about Jacques's financial affairs at the moment, but she kept her suspicions to herself.

"You look beautiful, Mrs. Clinton." Tom stood in front of her, his eyes taking in her slender form admiringly.

"Thanks." She stood on tiptoe and kissed him. "You look stunning yourself."

The party was at the home of an Italian banker turned film producer, and Paula remembered Simone's words about the financial and theater communities mixing. It must be the same party then. Expensive sports cars lined the driveway as red-coated valets scurried to whisk the vehicles out of sight behind the mansion.

"Is this going to be one of those affairs I've read about?" Paula asked as they inched forward toward the front of the house. "*La Dolce Vita* or whatever?"

"You mean an orgy? I certainly hope so. I've never been to one." Tom squeezed her hand reassuringly. "But I think it's highly unlikely."

"What if I make a mistake?" She wondered if it was the possibility of seeing movie stars that made her so nervous.

"Just keep doing what you've been doing since you became Mrs. Clinton, and you'll be fine," he said.

What I've been doing, she realized painfully, is falling in love with you. And I don't know how I'm going to get out of that.

She decided not to think about it.

It became evident the moment they walked through the door that this party bore little resemblance to the subdued one at Jacques d'Armand's estate.

The Mediterranean-style villa was built around a circular courtyard, in the midst of which played a fountain shaped like a nymph. Water splashed from its mouth, the sound refreshing against the heat that lingered in the night air.

Sensuous dance rhythms issued from a small band of dark-skinned musicians. Not a violin among them, Paula observed.

The people who swirled through the house amid the clink of cocktail glasses gave an impression of youth, although on closer examination the age range was rather wide.

Many women wore revealing dresses with cutouts in unlikely places. The men favored casual suits, and Paula spotted several wearing sunglasses, although the sun had gone down an hour ago.

A stocky man with a florid face greeted them, and Paula gathered that he was their host. His name didn't mean anything to her, but then, she wasn't very knowledgeable about Italian film making.

As she and Tom were led about for introductions, she gazed into the crowd, hoping to spot celebrities. There were a couple of women whom she thought she recognized from small roles in American movies, but that was all. There was no sign of Simone.

Paula accepted a brandy from the bar, her spirits soaring in spite of herself. She loved being here with Tom, loved moving as an equal among these sophisticated people, loved being addressed as Mme. Clinton.

She glanced at Tom. His eyes were bright and his cheeks flushed with exhilaration. So he was enjoying it, too.

The conversations they joined were mostly in English, which seemed to be the international language. Paula talked with the wives of Tom's acquaintances and found once again that rapport was easily achieved.

At the same time, she kept one ear cocked to overhear the glamorous references made by people nearby. Eavesdropping turned out to be an amusing pastime, as everyone seemed to be busy trying to impress each other. She caught snippets and phrases:

"Naturally, my agent told him I couldn't possibly..."

"...of course, they offered me the role first but I..."

"...on location in Egypt..."

"...when I get back from California."

Odd to think that the home state she took for granted represented glamour here.

However, the people Tom joined talked of mergers and interest rates, not movie deals and locations. Paula had to admire how comfortably he fit in with this cosmopolitan crowd; she hoped she didn't look too out of place.

Then she spotted Simone entering the courtyard.

Madame d'Armand's blond coolness contrasted sharply with the dark, exotic looks of the woman beside her, who was also considerably younger. That must be Melina, Paula guessed. What had Jacques called her? A crazy Greek actress.

The Mediterranean beauty was clad in a red dress fashioned of net, with glittering sequins covering only minimal areas. Paula thought for a moment that Melina might be wearing a body stocking, but no; most of her ripe figure was bare to the gaze.

Tom was staring at her. All the men were. How could they help it? Paula reflected with a touch of annoyance.

Then Simone noticed them, and the two women strolled over, Melina's eyes studying Tom with interest as her hips swayed in time to the music. A samba, Paula noted irrelevantly.

"Good evening," Simone said and made introductions.

"A pleasure to meet you." In a gallant gesture,

Tom bent to kiss the back of Melina's hand, his face perilously close to that oversize bosom. Paula could have pinched him.

Other couples joined them, and after a few minutes Tom asked Simone to dance. When she declined, he asked Melina, who agreed with obvious pleasure.

He has to be polite, Paula told herself, trying to keep from showing her jealousy as the two of them walked away together.

She helped herself to a glass of champagne from a waiter's tray. "Your friend is lovely," she told Simone.

The blond woman laughed. "A bit overblown, perhaps. Jacques can't stand her. But she has a good heart."

Yes, and it's well protected under that enormous chest, Paula thought spitefully, and then chided herself for her pettiness. "You look beautiful tonight."

Dressed in a form-fitting blue gown, Simone could have stepped from the pages of a fashion magazine. The dark circles were gone from her face, but there was an air of sadness in her eyes and she had a way of instinctively glancing about the room from time to time. Looking for Jacques?

The music changed. Forsaking Latin rhythms, the band launched into an exotic melody that hinted of Scheherazade.

From an interior room, a woman snaked through the crowd. Titian-haired and veiled, she wore an embroidered halter and low-cut harem pants with diaphanous legs.

A belly dancer! What fun! Paula thought, stepping back with the others to give the woman room to thread her way around the fountain. Tom, she noticed unhappily, was standing with Melina on the other side.

The dancer snapped her bracelets together, sending up a cymbal-like jangling. Appreciative whistles and calls sounded from the watchers.

The music intensified, and the woman swayed around the fountain, her stomach and hips enticing the men, her eyelashes trembling flirtatiously above the veil.

Her name was probably Sally Schwartz from Brooklyn, Paula told herself with a grin, but what a show she put on! In spite of the sexual innuendoes, the performer maintained a discreet distance that made it clear she was not available for any private encounters.

Paula glanced at Tom. He was laughing, one arm around Melina's midriff. It didn't mean anything, she told herself firmly. It was just his talent for fitting in with whatever situation arose.

But it hurt, too, to realize how readily he adjusted to a different companion. Paula had felt that the empathy between the two of them was special, but apparently Tom didn't think so.

The tingling sound of bells died away, and the belly dancer took her bows. Cheers went up, and the guests clamored for more as the woman darted off.

"Encore! Encore!" several men cheered lustily, but the dancer gave no sign of returning.

"La musique!" A demand went up for the band to resume the Mideastern strains, in hopes of luring back the performer. Obediently, the musicians filled the night with their sinuous melody, but the woman gave no sign of returning.

Melina took up the challenge. Snapping her fingers above her head, she moved into the cleared circle around the fountain. The crowd yelled encouragement.

Here was no hired dancer, no street girl pretending to be an exotic princess, but a true Greek beauty who carried with her an aura of instinctive seduction.

Melina's hips and stomach swayed suggestively. Clearly she'd had training; but then, that wouldn't be unusual for an actress.

And she was certainly putting her soul into it. As the onlookers beamed with delight, Melina insinuated herself around the courtyard.

Seminude breasts, belly, thighs wove through the moonlight. Crossing in front of Tom, Melina held out her arms and drew him into the circle with her.

He flung off his jacket and placed his hands on her scantily covered waist. The crowd murmured its response.

Paula could hardly breathe. The music was heavy, like a net entrapping her, imprisoning everyone except the enchanted pair dancing around the fountain. Tom was just having a good time, she told herself, wishing tears didn't prickle rebelliously at the back of her eyelids.

What did Simone think about all this? Paula glanced at her friend and saw the woman glaring in Melina's direction.

The brunette actress looked up and caught the reproachful gaze. She gave a little shrug, as if to say she hadn't meant any harm, and leaped gracefully onto the rim of the fountain.

In that elevated position, she moved away from Tom, still undulating to the appreciation of the men and the somewhat envious amusement of the women.

Melina hesitated in front of Paula. Then the Greek woman smiled apologetically and reached out, inviting the American to dance with her.

Well, why not? Paula thought. I can be a good sport about this.

And besides, she decided as she kicked off her high heels and jumped up beside Melina, if this is the kind of woman Tom likes, I'll show him I'm just as good as she is.

The musicians continued to play as Melina showed Paula how to shake her hips seductively. The others in the crowd shouted encouragement.

Paula sneaked a look at Tom. He was frowning. Well, it served him right.

After a minute she decided she had the hang of it and followed Melina as the actress circulated around the fountain. Exhilaration lifted Paula's spirits as the music filled her, and she responded with uninhibited rotations.

Then she slipped.

There must have been a wet spot on the fountain's rim. Whatever it was, Paula teetered helplessly for a second and tumbled into the water.

A roar of laughter went up from the watchers, but Paula was aware only of a surge of humiliation and the shock of cold washing through her thin dress.

And Tom's strong arms, pulling her out spluttering and choking.

"What the hell did you think you were doing?" His fingers bit into her arm.

Paula could only stare at him in dismay. Her hair clung to her neck like damp seaweed, and she was acutely aware of what a spectacle she'd made of herself.

"Are you all right?" It was Simone. "You'd better dry off, or you'll catch cold."

Their host produced a beach towel, and Paula did

her best to blot the soaked fabric as Tom fumed. Then, after a hasty farewell, he stalked from the house with her in tow.

Well, so much for Mr. and Mrs. Clinton's friendly arrangement, she thought, her emotions knocking against one another painfully.

They rode home in silence. Had she really ruined everything? she wondered miserably. But Tom had started it, dancing suggestively with Melina in front of the crowd. How had he expected Paula to react? Or didn't he care?

When they reached the villa, he pushed her almost roughly toward the bedroom. "Change into something dry and then come out here," he snapped. "There are a few things we need to get straight."

Her heart sinking, Paula peeled off the damp dress, hung it in the bathroom, and changed into her robe. She took a deep breath before stepping into the living room.

In the lamplight, Tom's face was tight with anger. "Do you have any idea what your childish behavior may have done?" He stood across the room from her, making no move to come closer.

"I'm sorry. I only meant to show that I was a good sport." But Paula realized it wasn't entirely true. She'd been angry at him for flirting with Melina.

"Wonderful." Tom paced across the floor, keeping his distance from her. "So in front of Simone d'Armand you acted like a—"

"A what?" Paula's head came up, angrily. "And what about you, ripping off your jacket and dancing around? What do you suppose Simone thought about that?"

"Jacques would understand my behavior." His voice emerged in a low growl. "But you went too far, Paula."

"And I suppose it was all right for you to let that Greek woman practically seduce you in front of Simone and everybody!" The words came out before she could stop them.

"There's no place in my business dealings for your misplaced jealousy." Tom stopped pacing and stood with his legs slightly apart, as if about to attack. "Do you understand that, Miss Ward?"

Paula straightened her shoulders. "Yes. I understand."

"Do you?" This tightly leashed fury of his was more frightening than if he'd yelled at her. "I'm paying you—and quite well, I might add—to play the role of my wife. I expect you to do that, and to follow orders. No matter what I may do around, with, or to any other woman."

She felt as if he'd struck her. Furiously Paula fought back the tears; at least she had her pride left. "I apologize. I made the mistake of forgetting for a few minutes that I'm just the hired help. It won't happen again."

"Paula . . ." He ran one hand through his light-brown hair, rumpling it.

"Would you rather sleep on the couch tonight, or shall I?" she demanded.

"We're both sleeping in bed. Together." He reached toward her, but she twisted away. After a momentary deadlock, Tom turned and stalked into the bedroom.

Paula stood there shaking. With part of her mind, she knew that she and Tom had probably both said things they didn't mean. Arguments were like that.

But the only thing her heart knew was that Tom considered her merely one more accessory to the great gamble.

Paula wrapped her arms around herself and went

to stand at the window, gazing into the moonlit night.

She loved Tom. There was no point in kidding herself. Despite her best intentions, she'd taken a crazy gamble, and lost.

If she were a heroine in a movie, she'd pack her clothes and disappear. But from a practical standpoint, Paula didn't see how she was going to arrange transportation back to California in the middle of the night from a country where she didn't even speak the language.

She grabbed a comforter from the closet and lay down on the couch, giving way to tears at last.

CHAPTER
Nine

PAULA AWOKE ALONE on the couch, her back and neck aching from the lumpy cushions. Sunlight washed over her, and she realized she'd slept until midmorning.

A rustling from the kitchen reminded her that Marie was on the premises. The housekeeper must have seen her sleeping here and deduced that the couple had had a fight.

Embarrassed, Paula hurried into the bedroom. The bed was neatly made. Lying on the bedside table was a folded piece of paper with her name on it.

Inside, Tom had written tersely: "Gone to lunch. Back later."

He hadn't even bothered to wake her up.

No, Paula told herself, pulling off the robe and moving to the shower, that wasn't fair. Perhaps he was trying to be considerate in letting her sleep late.

The sting of hot water failed to wash away the hurt left from the previous night's encounter. She'd allowed herself to hope, in spite of her best resolve, that the two of them might share something that transcended this trip or even Tom's business interests entirely.

In the light of day, she conceded that she'd overreacted to a mild flirtation with Melina. Tom wasn't likely to get tangled up with an actress of whom Jacques disapproved.

But his behavior at the party served as a warning flag. Tom amused himself easily with whatever woman was at hand. Circumstances had thrown him and Paula together, and Tom wasn't averse to enjoying the situation, but it meant no more to him than did a half hour's dalliance with Melina.

How naive she'd been! Well, no point in sulking over it, Paula thought. As soon as he returned, she'd ask to fly home. Surely Tom could make convincing excuses to their hosts.

She dried her hair and pulled on slacks and a scoop-necked T-shirt before realizing she had nothing to do that day. She certainly didn't feel like hanging around here for hours, waiting for Tom to wander back in.

Impulsively, Paula sought out Marie, but the housekeeper had gone on an errand, leaving her young assistant behind.

"I'd like to do some sight-seeing in Nice," Paula said. "Is there a bus that runs by here?"

"Yes, but surely Madame prefers a car and driver," the girl replied. "I can get one for this afternoon."

"Thanks, but I'd rather not wait." Paula made mental notes while the maid gave instructions on getting into town.

Glad that she'd changed some money in Paris, Paula soon found herself on the bus, bumping along the road to Nice. The countryside was verdant, the Mediterranean a deep azure, and if her heart felt like a lump of lead, why should she let that bother her?

It was hard to believe she'd been in France less than a week. So much had happened: she and Tom becoming lovers, Jacques's unacceptable business proposal, Simone's unhappiness, the escapade with Melina, and then the quarrel. Resolutely, Paula wrenched her thoughts back to the present.

Following instructions, she descended at the main bus station and proceeded to the Masséna Museum on the Promenade des Anglais, which ran along the water. On her way, Paula passed a park where elderly French men and women gossiped in the sunshine, looking like cast members for a production of *Gigi*.

Inside the museum, she took her time examining the artifacts of Napoleon's family, then proceeded to study the works of artists who had lived in the area—lighthearted Dufy and the more reflective Monet and Renoir.

After coffee and a sandwich at a sidewalk café, she abandoned her cultural intentions and poked through the shops along the main boulevards and in the old section of the city.

In one boutique, Paula found a tiny bikini in a golden color that made her skin glow. She also bought a silk scarf, perfume for her mother and Sally, an Italian wallet for her father, and a daring pink dress.

She settled down for more coffee before returning to the villa. Tom would like the bikini. And the dress.

Then she remembered that he'd probably never see them. Most likely Paula would be heading home on the first available plane.

She finished her cup of coffee in glum silence and made her way to the bus station.

Since she didn't have a watch, Paula hadn't bothered to check the schedule. Fortunately, she found that she had to wait only twenty minutes, but already the afternoon was almost gone.

Nestled among her packages as the bus rattled westward, she tried to ignore a twinge of apprehension. She'd been gone longer than she'd expected. Would Tom be angry with her for taking off without his permission?

Even cleaning ladies get a day off, she thought defiantly. I deserved a chance to do some shopping.

She stalked up the driveway, scarcely noticing the bulk of her parcels as her mind buzzed ahead. In the twilight, she saw the rental car sitting in front of the house. So he was home.

Paula stepped onto the porch, and Tom flung the door open, his eyes dark with anger. "I expect an explanation. And fast."

"For what?" She ignored his black look and walked inside.

"For pulling a disappearing act on me!" He slammed the door, making them both jump. "At first I thought you'd run off, until I noticed your clothes were still here."

"I went into Nice. Didn't the maid tell you?"

"Marie said she hadn't spoken with you." Paula thought she detected a note of uncertainty creeping into his voice.

"Not Marie. The other girl, the young one who helps her." Paula dumped her packages on the couch. "She gave me directions. I figured she'd pass the word along."

Tom leaned against the doorframe, his expression unreadable. "She must have left without saying anything. I didn't realize she'd even been in today, and Marie must not have thought of it either."

"Well, here I am." Paula straightened and met his gaze.

To her surprise, he lowered his eyes apologetically. "I...I'm sorry I lost my temper. I said some unpleasant things to you last night, things I didn't mean. That's why I thought you'd left."

He'd been worried, Paula realized with a shock.

"And...I'm awfully glad you're back. Forgive me?"

Feeling a small burst of happiness, Paula nodded. "Any word from Jacques today?"

"No. I guess Simone hasn't told him about you playing mermaid in the fountain." Tom grinned wryly. "And somehow he's restrained himself from coming up with a better offer."

Probably worried about his wife, Paula thought. In her heart she suspected that if only Jacques could bring himself to respect Simone as a full human being, things would go better for the couple. But Tom wouldn't be interested in that. "Your lunch wasn't with anyone helpful?"

"Just more smoke screen for Jacques's sake," Tom said. "I—frankly, I was already beginning to get discouraged, and then I came home and found that you'd run off. Even without your clothes, there's no telling what you might do."

"Even without my clothes?" She raised an eyebrow teasingly.

"That wasn't exactly what I meant but..." Tom traced a finger across her cheek. "Forgiven? Really?"

Paula nodded, swallowing the unexpected lump in her throat. She couldn't bear to leave this man a moment sooner than necessary, in spite of her earlier resolve to fly home. "I hope my escapade doesn't screw things up with Jacques. I'd hate to have caused something like that."

"Apparently Simone isn't as easily offended as her

husband." He gestured toward her packages. "What's all this?"

"Oh, Tom!" Paula bounced up, delighted at the thought of showing off her purchases. "Wait until you see what I bought. You'll love it."

"I want a personal fashion show."

"Coming right up." Paula whisked into the bedroom and put on the pink dress with its close-fitting bodice and flowing skirt. She selected a pair of black sandals and paraded back into the living room.

Tom looked at her admiringly. "Gorgeous. Let me check that out. We wouldn't want you to wear anything that doesn't fit properly."

Obediently, Paula held still while he made a pretense of checking how the dress fit her shoulders, bust, waist, and hips. The touch of his hands left her feeling light-headed and silvery.

"What about your other acquisitions?" he murmured. "I certainly hope you didn't stock up on overcoats."

Paula darted away and returned with the silk scarf. She held it across her nose and mouth, harem-style, and batted her eyes.

"Wrong ethnic group," Tom teased. "Arabian concubines don't have blue eyes."

"I'm a Scandinavian princess who was kidnapped by pirates and sold into slavery," she improvised.

He chuckled and leaned back on the couch. "I hope you're about to perform the dance of the seven veils, using only one veil."

"Not quite." She lowered the scarf. "But I do have something else to show you."

She took her time in the bedroom, putting on the bikini. Unable to forget the tantalizing lushness of

Melina's body through the net dress, Paula wanted to look her best.

Fresh lipstick and powder didn't seem like enough, so she added a delicate chain about one ankle and a tiny heart necklace around her throat. Regarding herself in the mirror, she thought: I may not look exotic, but I certainly don't look like the cleaning lady.

Paula swung open the door dramatically and posed in the doorway like a calendar model.

Tom's eyes sparkled, and he stood up. "I'm not sure how well that's made. I'd better give it a closer inspection."

"Oh, no, that simply isn't permitted." She backed through the doorway in mock horror. "You mustn't touch the merchandise."

"But it's my responsibility," Tom protested, following her into the bedroom. "If the swimsuit isn't made properly, you'll have to take it back. I'm just trying to save you a lot of trouble."

"Out of the question!" She moved around the bed, challenging him with a pout. "The models are not available for inspection."

"But I work here." Tom advanced relentlessly. "I'm the official bikini checker on the premises."

Paula had reached the French windows and found them unlatched. She fumbled with one hand behind her back. "You don't look like a couturier. Are you sure you aren't one of the window dressers?"

"Perhaps I could use you in an unusual display I have in mind." He feigned a leer. "Now if you'll just let me . . ."

The window came open. Giggling, Paula dashed outside and through the greenery toward the secluded pool.

"Come back here!" Tom chased after her. "Honest, I just want to be sure you haven't thrown your money away."

"You can examine me from a distance." She hopped around a deck chair.

"It wouldn't be the same." He paused, watching her like a tiger stalking its prey, the chair between them.

Paula glanced about. In the twilight, a bark-strewn path disappeared from sight between tall ferns. She had no idea where it led, but this seemed as good a time as any to find out.

With a whoop, she sped along the path, hearing Tom's footsteps thumping closer and closer. Strong arms clasped her as she burst upon wooden decking that held a hot tub.

She uttered a shriek and tried to scuttle backward between his legs, but he held her fast.

"Now let's see about that bikini."

"You can't view it properly in this position." Paula was almost doubled over, half under him. She peeked up through her tangled hair.

"All right." One hand clamped firmly on her arm, Tom let her straighten up in front of him. "Do I have your word that there will be no more shenanigans by the model? This is a business we're running here, you know."

"I'm sure you'll be fully satisfied with the way the bikini fits, sir." She held herself erect as Tom began his mock inspection.

"The straps seem sturdy enough." He tested them across Paula's squared shoulders. "Turn, please."

She obeyed and felt him try the elastic in back. His touch tickled a little, deliciously.

Then he spun her around and ran his thumbs along the edge of the bra, stroking the swell of her breasts. "It does display an acceptable amount of cleavage," he confirmed.

"I knew you'd be pleased, sir." She continued in her role as model.

Tom's hands ventured lower, across the vulnerable curve of her stomach to the line of the bikini bottom, dangerously low over her hips. Then down to her thighs.

"Does everything meet with your approval?" she said.

"Well, I'm a little unhappy with the way this top fits." Tom frowned in pretended concentration. "Let me take another look."

With unexpected swiftness, he reached around, unhooked it, and lifted the bra away, exposing her breasts to the warm evening air.

"Tom!" Paula crossed her arms in front of her. "Somebody might see!"

"Who? Marie? I gave her the evening off to go visit her sister in Cannes." Tom tossed the bikini top onto a lounge chair. "Anyway, don't tell me you're inhibited about a little public nudity."

Paula couldn't remember when she'd ever been undressed outdoors before; certainly not since she was a child. Yet this was a completely private setting.

"I'll tell you what"—Tom unbuttoned his shirt—"We're both in this together."

"You're not serious!"

"I've always loved a good hot tub in the buff, particularly out of doors." He removed his shirt, followed by his shoes and socks.

Paula slowly lowered her arms and watched as the

rest of his clothing was tossed onto the same lounge chair. The last rays of the sun rippled across his bronze skin.

The sight of his strikingly masculine body bare in this leafy glade released the last of her inhibitions. Paula drew off the bottom to her suit and saw a smile light his face.

"I knew we were two of a kind," Tom said softly.

Reaching for her hand, he drew her into the sunken hot tub. The water was pleasantly warm, not overheated, and for a while they relaxed in silence.

Then Tom flicked on the jets, and water spurted around them, massaging away the soreness of a tension-filled day.

Paula rested her head against the edge of the pool and closed her eyes. The air was beginning to cool, forming a stimulating contrast to the heated water.

Through the steam, she looked up at the stars. The same ones she saw from California, of course. Yet how far away she was, in the midst of unforeseen adventures. And despite her doubts, Tom was still with her.

Their gazes met across the hot tub, and he moved to her side.

"I was watching you." He touched her shoulder lightly. "So many emotions rippling across your face. I wish I could read your mind."

"It's X-rated," Paula whispered.

"Oh?" His hand moved over her breasts. The touch was incredibly erotic, amid the sensations of heat and cold and the unfamiliar experience of being naked in the open air.

Paula ran her hands up Tom's chest, feeling how the water beaded and clung to the curly hair. She explored him eagerly, tracing the firm line of his jaw with its hint of stubble, following the muscular length of his arms, then nibbling at his throat and collarbone.

They stretched alongside each other in the water, half floating, their bodies bumping lightly.

The spray jets surrounded them with movement and sound, adding to the sense that the world ceased to exist beyond this spot. The only light came from the moon and from small fixtures imbedded in the tub.

Tom caught Paula's hips and pulled her closer. Skin against skin, without pretense or subterfuge. She could feel his readiness for her, and her own for him.

Neither of them wanted to hurry this moment, this treasured time of solitude and closeness beneath the Mediterranean sky.

Then the urgency of Tom's desire overcame his reluctance, and he began to twist beneath her, bringing her breasts tight against his chest, his legs tangling between hers.

Eager lips found her mouth. His tongue parted the gateway and plunged inside, tantalizing, possessing.

Paula felt herself lifted half out of the water. Her skin prickled cool in the moonlight, and then his mouth closed over her straining nipples and she gasped in pleasure.

Sitting on the low shelf inside the hot tub, Tom lowered her onto his lap and kissed her again. Then he paused, staring gravely into her face.

"Tom?" She could hardly speak in her hunger for him.

"So beautiful." He hugged her close and, with an upward thrust, completed their union.

Their bodies flowed together, floating through time

and space and delirium. Paula clung to his shoulders, afraid not so much of drowning as of being swept away from him.

They explored each other and the water at the same time, tingling with the novelty of the experience and reveling in their oneness.

Tom carried her into a passionate dream of cascades and whirlpools. Paula writhed against him, urging him on, yearning for fulfillment and yet wanting to prolong this surge of ecstasy.

They could wait no longer. A tide of desire swept them along, faster and faster, until they burst over a waterfall together, tumbling and crying out and laughing at the same time.

And then, still unwilling to release each other, they drifted in the heat and the night, holding fast.

At last Paula let herself float away, bubbles circulating across her sensitized skin.

"I always wondered what it would be like, making love in a hot tub." Tom stretched out lazily. "It was better than I ever fantasized."

He looked splendid, relaxing there with his arms resting along the rim of the tub, his well-muscled body glowing from the exertion of lovemaking.

Paula let the water buoy her as she hovered in the center of the pool. "I'd think, with your wealth, that you'd have carried out every one of your fantasies long ago."

"Not all fantasies are as"—he searched for the right word—"self-indulgent as lounging in hot tubs."

Was that how Tom saw women, as leisure-time playthings separate from the real business of living, or was she making too much of his comment? she wondered.

Paula swam over and cuddled against him, pushing aside the concerns that threatened to intrude. She was going to enjoy every moment she could with Tom.

"What are we going to do now?" she asked at last.

"Stay here all night."

Paula laughed. "That isn't what I meant."

A brief pause, then he said, "I have one more lunch meeting tomorrow. It's a long shot, but perhaps he'll make an offer."

"And if not?"

"Unless I miss my guess, Jacques should be here this weekend," Tom said. "That's our last chance. If it doesn't work out, we go home."

"Then what will you do?" She studied him with concern.

Across his face slanted a shadow that she remembered seeing before. Was he really so frightened of losing his business? Maybe he'd run up debts beyond the company's resources, she speculated.

"Well, you know us gamblers," he said with forced lightness. "We never quit."

The words chilled her, more than she wanted him to know. Oh, she knew about gamblers only too well.

A quarter of an hour later, they were both beginning to feel prunelike and ready to retreat.

"No towels," Paula said.

Tom looked around. "You're right. Well?"

The exchanged glances and, with one thought, clambered out of the pool and snatched up their garments from the chairs. Leaving pools of water along the path, they scampered back to the haven of their room.

CHAPTER
Ten

THE NEXT MORNING, they slept late and Paula stayed in bed until Tom left for his breakfast meeting. Marie arrived with a breakfast tray and explained that she took Friday afternoons off.

"There's a salad in the refrigerator, if you like," the housekeeper assured her.

"Thanks." From under the covers, Paula watched her go, feeling a bit embarrassed. The woman no doubt thought Paula lounged in bed until noon every day. What would she think if she knew the usual regime was up at six and cleaning duty by seven?

But I might as well take it easy, Paula reminded herself as she bit into a flaky croissant. It would be a long time before she got to take another paid vacation.

She listened as Marie's car pulled out of the driveway. For a moment it sounded as if there were two engines, but that must be an echo. Marie's old jalopy lacked a muffler and made enough noise for half a dozen automobiles.

What finally got Paula out of bed was the sight of

her bikini lying on the floor.

She'd been longing to try nude sunbathing, and last night had shown this was the perfect place for it. With Marie gone, there was no one to be scandalized. Wouldn't Sally be envious if Paula came back with an all-over tan!

Smiling to herself, she hopped up, donned the bikini, and took a towel out to the pool area.

Satisfied that there was no one around, she undressed, tossed the swimsuit and towel on a chair, and lay face down on a chaise longue.

It took more courage than she would have expected to turn over and brown her front. She couldn't help peering up at the cloudless sky as though she feared a helicopter might appear and take photographs.

Paula smiled to herself. It was a good thing she wasn't a movie star. She doubted anyone would pay for nude photos of her even if someone did take them.

She shut her eyes and let the sun beat down across her breasts and thighs, remembering how the water had flowed over her as she and Tom made love the night before.

It seemed impossible that such a man really existed. Maybe she'd dreamed him. Maybe she'd wake up and find that she'd simply fallen asleep on the beach at Balboa and none of this had ever really happened.

I don't want to wake up, Paula thought.

At that moment, a shoe crunched gravel on the path.

Her eyes flew open. It was too soon for Tom to be back... unless his lunch meeting had been canceled.

She flipped onto her stomach and peered up. Standing there with a surprised expression on his face was

Jacques d'Armand, clad in a lightweight business suit.

"Oh, hello." Paula felt herself blushing to the tips of her toes as she grabbed for the towel and wrapped it quickly around herself. "I . . . uh . . . wasn't expecting anyone."

"So I see." He maintained his composure, but kept his eyes politely averted. "Your husband is away?"

"He . . . had a business meeting. He should be back after lunch." Tom would want to see Jacques, she felt sure, but she could hardly play hostess wrapped in a towel!

"I should have called to let you know I was coming." Jacques still wasn't looking directly at her. "I hadn't intended to arrive until the weekend, but some matters came up unexpectedly."

Simone? Paula wondered. She hoped Jacques's trip meant he was trying to win his wife back.

"Just let me change into something more modest," she said, rising carefully and scooping up her bikini with one hand. "I'd be honored if you'd join me for lunch. Marie left a salad in the refrigerator."

Jacques looked uncertain.

"Wait right there." Paula darted into the bedroom, ruing her luck. Why did she have to pick this day of all days to try nude sunbathing?

She put on a pair of slacks and a cotton sweater, then raced into the kitchen. Fortunately, Marie had left a pot of coffee on the warmer.

When Paula returned to the pool area carrying the food and coffee on a tray, Jacques was sitting on a canvas chair staring moodily into the pool.

"We've been enjoying your house," Paula said, hoping the blandness of the conversation would help Jacques forget the undoubtedly shocking sight of her nude body sprawled on the chaise longue.

He, too, seemed to prefer safe topics. "Have you had a chance to see much of our beautiful coast?"

"Some of it," Paula said. "I went shopping in Nice and saw the museum. What a beautiful city!"

"Ah, yes." He nodded sagely. "The Riviera is a special place. Each town is like a gem, with its own particular facets. Paris is a great diamond necklace, string after string of jewels, so dazzling that it becomes difficult to see the beauty of any one of them."

"How poetic," she said admiringly.

Jacques sipped his coffee and then asked, with what she thought was feigned disinterest, "Perhaps my wife has come by?"

"Yes, she dropped in for a visit just after we arrived." What was the harm of admitting the obvious? "And then we ran into them at a party."

"Them?" A slight narrowing of the eyes revealed his unease. Did Jacques think his wife was going out with another man?

"Simone and Melina," Paula said.

"Ah, yes, of course." He tapped one finger against the saucer. "So she's staying with Melina."

Paula suffered a pang of guilt. Jacques hadn't known where Simone was after all, and now she'd given it away. But then, she told herself, didn't he have a right to know? He'd have guessed sooner or later anyway.

Jacques was speaking again. "She's a bad influence, Melina. She lacks self-restraint."

"I guess so." Paula smiled inwardly at the memory of the actress gyrating around the fountain and wondered how Jacques would have reacted. "Her dress didn't leave much to the imagination."

"I don't know why Simone associates with her."

Because she's so different from the starchy people you hang around with, Paula thought, biting her lip against the words. "Are you going to be staying here with us?" she asked instead. "I know Tom would enjoy your company."

"Yes, for a day or so." Jacques looked up, and for the first time she noticed the fine lines around his eyes that hadn't been visible before. "Perhaps my wife will be joining us. If you'll excuse me, I'll telephone and tell her I'm here."

"Of course." Paula watched as the Frenchman strode into the house, his figure rigidly erect beneath the expensive summer suit.

Had he always been this demanding? It was hard to imagine a youthful Simone falling in love with Jacques. But on the other hand, he possessed some qualities Paula herself valued very highly: dependability, stability, love for his family.

A few minutes later, the sound of Tom's car in the driveway brought a rush of relief. He'd be glad to see Jacques again—although it didn't seem likely the Frenchman had spent much time thinking about business deals these past few days.

Carrying the tray, Paula reentered the house to find Tom and Jacques together.

"There you are." Tom kissed the top of Paula's head in his most husbandly manner. "Jacques has invited us to join him and Simone for dinner tonight. I said that would be most agreeable."

"Of course." Paula slipped her arm through his. What had happened during the telephone conversation? Were the husband and wife reconciled or had Jacques merely insisted that Simone attend the dinner?

Jacques carried his suitcase to a room at the far

side of the house. Then, to Paula's relief, he left for a few hours, saying he had calls to make.

"We'd better be careful," Tom said after their host was gone. "Things could get awkward, staying in this place with him. The walls are a lot thinner than in his Paris house."

Paula followed Tom into the bedroom and waited while he changed into casual slacks and an open-necked shirt. "How did your lunch meeting go?" she asked.

He dropped into a chair. "The bankers around here feel the computer business is too volatile. That's probably what they said about the invention of the wheel."

"Jacques must be interested," she mused. "Why else would he have invited us for dinner tonight?"

"Sadism?"

She laughed, then sobered quickly as she remembered the scene at the swimming pool. "Tom . . . Jacques walked in on me while I was sunbathing nude. I covered up right away, and he didn't make a big deal out of it, but I thought you should know. I hope I haven't caused more problems."

"I doubt it." He didn't look in the least upset. "Tanning in the altogether is a popular pastime around here, and there's nothing morally wrong with a respectable married woman doing it in private. I doubt if he'll attach any importance to it."

"Looking back, it must have been funny," she conceded. "Both of us turning beet-red and trying to pretend nothing had happened."

He chuckled, and she wondered whether to tell him about the rest of the conversation. This evening he'd certainly notice something amiss, wouldn't he?

Briefly, Paula described the situation between

Jacques and Simone, as she had deduced it over the days.

Tom listened with a frown. "Sounds to me like you're turning into everybody's confidante."

"Not at all," Paula defended herself. "Mostly I read between the lines."

"Don't forget why we're here," he warned. "What's between Jacques and Simone is their affair, and they're both old enough to take care of their own problems. Don't interfere."

"Aren't you even concerned?" she asked, looking askance. "Don't you care about anybody but yourself? Or about anything except money?"

"Is that what you think of me?" Tom's eyes met hers in astonishment. "Paula, believe me. I have good reasons for trying to save Clinton Computers. Beyond mere . . . greed."

"What reasons?" Please tell me, she prayed. Please show me that you're not totally self-absorbed, consumed with winning, with money. Like Mickey, she added silently.

Instead, he said, "They're private. Now let's go have a glass of wine."

Paula sat motionless for a moment after he left the room. Private. Too private to tell her. Who was she, anyway? Just a woman who happened to be in love with him.

Determined not to show her hurt, she trailed after him, and tried to keep the conversation impersonal for the rest of the day.

Jacques returned at seven o'clock to change and take them to dinner. As his automobile was a two-seater, they took the larger rental car.

The town of St-Paul-de-Vence is located in the mountains that rise just inland of the coastal plain. A picturesque town, it is known—as Jacques explained—for its modern art gallery and for its cuisine.

They parked on one of the narrow streets and walked to the town's distinguished restaurant, located in the courtyard of an old mansion. Tables had been set out of doors, and the hum of voices and the clink of china filled the air.

Paula had assumed there would be four of them at dinner, but when they entered the courtyard they saw half a dozen people sitting around a long table to one side.

Melina looked stunning in a black dress with a deeply slashed V neck. Beside her sat Simone—a very different Simone from the one Paula had met before.

Blond hair fell loose around her shoulders, and she gestured with animation as she talked to the middle-aged man across from her. Apparently a few days away from her husband had shaken free some of her inhibitions.

Then Simone looked up and spotted Jacques. The conversation at the table dwindled.

Simone rose and moved coolly across the courtyard, giving her husband a restrained peck on the cheek. "I hope you don't object; some of the other cast members are joining us."

"No, of course I don't mind," he said stiffly.

Simone greeted Paula and Tom with more warmth and escorted them back to the table, where she introduced them to the other guests.

"So, you are recovered from the party?" Melina asked mischievously. "No permanent damage?"

At Jacques's quizzical look, Paula explained, "I had a little accident."

"It was my fault," Melina added quickly, apparently realizing that she'd put Paula in an embarrassing situation. "I was belly dancing and tried to teach Madame Clinton. She was a good sport, and what did I do? Clumsy me, I knocked her into the fountain."

Paula shot the actress a grateful look.

Simone had resumed her former seat, leaving Jacques to find a place at the far end of the table. He made no comment, but glanced at her from time to time with a puzzled expression.

Why can't he see what's so obvious to everyone else? Paula mused. But then, I suppose we all have trouble seeing clearly the things that are closest to our hearts.

The dinner proved delicious, the dishes garnished with exquisite sauces and accompanied by a superb wine. But Paula's enjoyment was tempered by her awareness of the subtle tension between husband and wife.

Melina kept the talk swirling around the theater group and its upcoming productions, speaking English out of consideration for their guests. Jacques kept quiet except to urge the lavish food on Tom and Paula, and remark that he rarely had time to go to amusements.

Amusements. At the word, Simone frowned and then pointedly turned away.

"Would anyone like dessert?" Jacques asked and, without waiting for an answer, signaled the waiter to bring the dessert tray.

The display of intricate pastries and mousse pies overwhelmed Paula's best dietary intentions. "Maybe just a small one..."

Jacques ordered a large selection for the table. By the time they finished, Paula felt as if she might burst.

Back to dieting with a vengeance when she got home, she thought.

One of the other men addressed Jacques. "I can't tell you how pleased we are that your wife will be joining us. She was astounding yesterday at the read-through."

That must mean they'd been reading the script aloud before beginning rehearsals, Paula thought.

Everything about Jacques tightened—his shoulders, neck, jaw. "There seems to be some misunderstanding," he said. "My wife is only visiting her friend. She is not joining the theater group."

"There is no misunderstanding," Simone rejoined. "I'm staying here until October, Jacques."

His cold stare made Paula shiver, and even Simone looked somewhat daunted. "A wife belongs with her husband. If you wish to be released from your marriage vows, I have no choice but to oblige."

Paula stifled a gasp. Jacques must really be furious, to carry on this quarrel in public. Or perhaps he realized that, by issuing his ultimatum in front of witnesses, he was forcing Simone to make a choice.

"Jacques..." The blond woman hesitated. "Must everything be black and white? Don't I have any right to a life of my own?"

"You can have any kind of life you wish." He stood up, putting an end to the conversation. "If our guests will excuse me, I think my digestion would benefit from a walk before we leave."

He strode away, leaving a stunned silence behind. Paula guessed that this was his way of giving Simone a few minutes to think. But what a cruel choice he was forcing on her!

"Maybe I can talk to him," Paula volunteered,

jumping up and evading Tom's grasp.

She hurried to catch up with Jacques, following him out of the courtyard and down a neighboring street. The town was hilly, and Paula teetered slightly on her high heels.

"Paula?" Jacques turned, surprised, and waited for her to catch up.

"I... needed to stretch my legs," she said as she came abreast of him. "Do you mind?"

"Of course not. It is a pleasure." He spoke the words formally, his mind clearly occupied elsewhere.

Paula couldn't concentrate on the quaint houses or the starry bowl of the sky as they resumed the walk. He was too busy trying to figure out how to begin.

Finally she gave up and took the direct approach. "Jacques, I know this is none of my business, but I think Simone loves you very much."

"You are young and newly married," Jacques said gently as they turned along a side street. "You see everything through the eyes of a girl in love. Things are not like that between Simone and me."

"Weren't you ever in love?" she asked.

Jacques's gray eyes grew thoughtful. "Yes, naturally, but these things change as the years go by. There are children to consider, and other relatives, and one's social contacts. Love cannot remain the same."

"No, I suppose not," Paula agreed. "But maybe what you end up with is even better. Less... unexpected, but deeper."

"That is so, in the best cases," Jacques said. "But if that does not happen, then one must simply make the best of things. Not run away."

Paula hated to argue with him, afraid that he'd withdraw from this highly personal conversation. She suspected that, like many men, Jacques had no one but his wife with whom to discuss emotional matters. It was probably out of desperation that he was opening up to her this way.

"I thought that too, at first," she said carefully. "That Simone was running away. But I decided I was wrong."

"Why?" It was hard to read Jacques's expression in the moonlight, but at least he was listening.

"At the party where I saw her, she kept glancing around the room as if expecting to see someone," Paula said. "I remembered that at your party she did that, too, and the person she was looking for was you."

"That is mere habit," he said. "If she loved me, she wouldn't consider leaving me."

"Jacques, Simone is going through something that happens to many women," Paula said. "Raising a family is a woman's job, just as you have your own work."

"Yes, of course." He slowed his pace instinctively to allow her to keep up.

"Well, now that your daughters are grown, she's lost her job—been laid off, so to speak," Paula pressed on. "Playing hostess for you and being a mother whenever the children visit home isn't a full-time occupation."

Jacques shook his head. "There are many things she could do to fill the time. I never objected to charity work."

Talking to him was like trying to bail out a boat with a teaspoon, Paula reflected in frustration, but she wouldn't give up.

"That's just it," she said. "I suspect that Simone

doesn't want just to fill the time. She wants a job that means something to her, that's emotionally rewarding. She probably believes she can have you and the theater, both."

"A woman doesn't walk out on the man she loves," he said. "I look at you and remember what things were like long ago. I think you would do anything for Tom, no?"

"Well, anything within reason," she joked, relieved that he didn't resent her interference. "It's not as if we were mar—"

She stopped, but it was too late.

Jacques's expression metamorphosed slowly into disbelief. "You're not married?"

Paula stared at him in dismay. "We're . . . I didn't mean . . ."

"I see." The man had turned to ice. "Now I understand why you are sympathetic with a runaway wife. To you I am just the stupid fool, the hoodwinked husband and the target of whatever game you and your . . . boyfriend are playing."

"No, honestly." The words tripped over each other. "It was an accident . . ."

But he didn't wait for her to finish. Torn by a sense of having betrayed the people who trusted her most, Paula watched helplessly as Jacques stalked away through the village.

CHAPTER

Eleven

PAULA HESITATED AT the entrance to the restaurant courtyard. Had she ruined any chance for a reconciliation between Jacques and Simone? And for Tom's loan, as well? What was Tom going to say?

The sound of an engine made her look up in time to see a taxi vanishing down the street. The ramrod-straight figure in the back seat was obviously Jacques.

Paula stepped forward to get a clear view of the table. Simone was in the midst of a rapid-fire conversation with her companions, and Tom was listening with a bemused expression. He didn't appear upset, and Paula realized that Jacques had not returned to the table. Instead he had left without so much as a farewell.

Uneasily she forced herself to walk casually across to join the others.

"Where's Jacques?" Tom asked, standing and holding a chair for her.

Paula sat down reluctantly. "He . . . decided to leave. He took a cab."

Even as the others continued their discussion, Simone met Paula's gaze across the table, and Paula looked at her glumly. The Frenchwoman pursed her lips and shrugged, as if to say that she'd always known her husband was quite impossible anyway.

"What's going on?" Tom muttered.

"I'm afraid I managed to make things worse." She couldn't tell him the bad news in front of the others.

"Frankly, after seeing Jacques's outburst, I'm not sure that's possible."

"Maybe we should leave now." Paula kept her tone low. "There's something I need to tell you."

After a moment's reflection, Tom stood up and made their excuses. He reached for his wallet, but Simone waved her hand.

"My husband already paid," she said. "Please, I hope to see you both before you leave France."

"I'd like that." Paula hoped she didn't look as distraught as she felt.

"What's going on?" Tom asked as soon as he started the motor. "Why did Jacques disappear like that?"

"Oh, Tom." Paula closed her eyes and leaned her head back on the seat.

"Maybe you'd better tell me what happened." He sounded grim.

"I—we were talking about marriage. He asked me something—I don't even remember what—and somehow I just let it slip." There; it was done.

"Jacques knows we're not married?" he said tensely.

"Yes," she said. "I'm sorry. I know you warned me about getting too close to these people. But I felt so bad about what was happening between him and Simone . . ."

Tom stared straight ahead as he eased the car down the curving mountain road. The silence itself was frightening as they descended to the coast and headed for Cap-Ferrat. Paula almost wished he would shout at her so she would know what he was thinking.

As mile after mile passed by without a word, her heart thumped inside her like a piece of coal on a string. Swing, bump, swing, bump. Heavy and black and dead.

She'd failed Tom, ruined the most important business deal of his life. By now, Paula knew where his priorities lay, knew that she came in a distant second to the millions he had hoped to net.

How could she have been so foolish? And what about Simone? If anything, Paula had confirmed Jacques's conviction that a respectable woman wouldn't behave as his wife had done.

She'd never felt so miserable in her life.

Jacques's sports car was gone from the driveway, she observed as they came to a halt. There was an odd sense of relief in knowing that at least she wouldn't have to face him right away.

Her nerves on edge waiting for Tom's explosion, Paula followed him into the house. He poured them each a glass of sherry from a decanter.

"I guess there's no point in saying I'm sorry." She sank limply onto the couch. "I've made a mess of everything."

Without speaking, Tom sat beside her.

"Well?" she demanded. "Aren't you going to let me have it with both barrels? Go on, get it over with. I can't stand this silent treatment."

Tom took a sip of his sherry. "I'm in shock."

"Uh-oh," she said. "That means I have to sweat it out until the numbness wears off?"

"No." He set his glass on the coffee table and

turned to face her. "I can't really blame you. This whole scheme was madness to begin with. I never would have attempted it except . . . well, it's my own fault. If I hadn't been so wrapped up in saving Clinton Computers . . ."

His voice trailed off sadly, and he shook his head. "I suppose we'd better start packing before Jacques throws us out of here on our ears."

"You're giving up?" She couldn't believe it, not after all they'd gone through.

"How can you reason with a man who'd throw aside his own wife, the woman he's raised two children with, because she won't devote the rest of her life to feeding his ego?" Tom said, rising.

Paula couldn't comprehend that she would escape without a thorough tongue-lashing. "But aren't you angry that I ran after him, when you didn't want me to?"

A ghost of a smile flitted across his face. "I only tried to stop you because I knew it was useless. I didn't realize how much trouble that marriage was in until that scene at dinner; and then I realized Jacques was too far gone in his own thinking to be helped. Paula, it's your nature to care about other people, even if you're too impulsive in the way you go about it. I can't hold that against you."

As he moved away into the bedroom, Paula thought this resigned, melancholy mood of his was harder to take than blind fury.

She felt as if she'd killed something deep inside the man she loved. Was there indeed something so very important about this business deal, something beyond the money involved? If only he'd tell her!

Well, whatever it was, she'd ruined his plans. Why

couldn't she stop herself from loving him even now, when he clearly had no further use for her?

Depressed, Paula went into the bedroom to change. Tom was sitting by the French doors, staring into the night.

"Is there anything I can do?" she asked.

He shook his head. "No, thanks. I think I'll go for a walk."

Without inviting her to come along, he slid open the doors and stepped out into the darkness.

Alone, Paula ached for him. Oh, Tom, I love you so much; why won't you reach out to me? Do I really mean that little to you? she wondered.

She crawled shivering between the covers and lay there, feeling empty and tormented by guilt. Sally had been right all along: Paula was in over her head when she tried to deal with Thomas C. Clinton III. It would be almost a relief to get back to the simple life of pushing a vacuum cleaner around.

Oh, yeah? muttered a voice from a forgotten corner of her brain. Things would have to get a lot worse before you looked forward to that!

After a few minutes she dozed off, awakening an indeterminate time later to hear masculine voices in the living room.

Paula hurried out of bed, pulling on her bathrobe before trundling into the living room.

Tom was standing there. And Jacques.

"Hi," said Paula.

The Frenchman gave her a brief, disapproving stare and turned back to Tom. "I will repeat, so your . . . girlfriend understands also, that I expect you to leave this house as early as possible tomorrow morning."

"We'll be gone as soon as I can get a flight out," Tom said coldly.

Jacques wasn't finished. "I didn't expect this in my own home. I will have a few strong words for the Jensens. It was their responsibility to screen you more carefully."

"I won't attempt to excuse our behavior," Tom replied. The men remained standing, and so did Paula, although she felt extremely awkward. "Except to say that there was no intention to embarrass you."

Jacques uttered a short, humorless laugh. "Embarrass me? Oh, certainly not. Merely inducing me to present you to my friends as a respectable married couple couldn't cause me any embarrassment."

Instead of arguing, Tom walked past him and took a seat on the couch. "There is one thing I want to tell you, Jacques. You have a right to know how this came about."

"It no longer concerns me." Their host remained standing.

"Sit down." Tom waved at a chair. "There's no point in our standing around."

With a sigh, Paula sat beside Tom, and after a moment, Jacques lowered himself reluctantly into the chair.

"Paula works for me," Tom said. "She's my cleaning lady."

"I beg your pardon?"

"My maid." Tom took another sip of sherry, giving the Frenchman time to absorb the shock. "She was changing her clothes in my bathroom when I came home with the Jensens unexpectedly. When they discovered that there was an unclad woman in the apartment, I knew they'd never believe the truth."

"If it is the truth," Jacques said.

"You prove my point." Tom remained unruffled, to Paula's amazement. "You don't believe it, and neither would they have. I don't excuse my dishonesty, nor am I asking your forgiveness. Matters between us have gone too far to be repaired. But I tell you this for a reason."

"If you think I can overlook your conduct..."

"Not at all. Our behavior has been questionable, and I take full blame," Tom went on. "Paula had no choice—unless she wanted to lose her job, which she couldn't afford to do. But it's the Jensens I want to talk to you about."

"I can deal with my partners myself," Jacques snapped, starting to rise.

"The way you deal with your wife?" Tom's comment drew a furious glare, but he pressed on. "Harsh, uncompromising people force others to make unreasonable choices. As the Jensens did with us. As I believe you're doing with Simone."

Paula couldn't believe it. Was he more concerned with helping Simone and Jacques than he was with trying to salvage his chances for the loan? It almost seemed so.

"This is intolerable!" Jacques drew himself up in fury. "First you try to hoodwink me, then you interfere in my private affairs!"

"Oh, Jacques, please don't let your anger with us get in the way of your feelings for Simone!" Paula said, half frightened of him but determined.

"My relationship with my wife is not up for discussion." He turned to leave, and impulsively she rose and darted in front of him.

"Simone loves you," Paula insisted. "I know you

feel hurt, but you've caused her even more pain because she doesn't think you love her."

"How would you know that?" At least he wasn't thrusting by her toward the door.

"It's something another woman can sense." Paula spoke from her heart, not sure at that moment how much of her own feeling she was voicing. "She thinks you don't care about her as a woman, as the person she is inside, but only as an empty shell—someone to entertain your friends and warm your bed."

"My wife understands what marriage is about," he rejoined, but he didn't sound quite so sure of himself. "She isn't a child."

"And neither are you!" Paula cried. "Do you have to have your own way in everything? Can't you compromise even a little, to show Simone that you want her to be happy?"

The Frenchman inhaled deeply, studying the troubled expression on the woman in front of him. "You may find this hard to believe, but I do try to be fair. I will admit that I spoke to you of my concerns about Simone, and perhaps that is why you feel you have a right to interfere."

Paula waited, holding her breath and fighting back the urge to plead further.

"And perhaps Monsieur Clinton has a point about the Jensens. They do not separate their personal standards from good business sense."

Tom, she noticed, remained sitting on the couch, but had swiveled to observe them.

"Frankly, it was my intention to make a second offer," Jacques said. "If you think I am unjust and incapable of compromise, I will prove you wrong. I am willing to discuss the offer with you, Mr. Clinton."

Paula held her breath. Was it possible that everything wasn't lost?

Tom's next words dashed her hopes. "Jacques, I appreciate your generosity, but you misunderstand me. I don't object to morality in business dealings, only to excessive inflexibility."

"You do not wish to discuss terms?" It was impossible to read the Frenchman's expression.

"No, I don't," Tom said. "It's obvious you hold Paula and me in such low esteem that any working relationship between us would be strained in the extreme. Nor do I think the Jensens would take to it kindly, not when they learn the truth. No, Jacques. I think it would be best for all concerned if Paula and I leave tomorrow, as planned."

Jacques bowed stiffly and went to his room.

"Tom," Paula began. "We're all tired and out of sorts. In the morning—"

"We're flying back to Los Angeles," he said. She caught a glimpse of his face, tired and grim, before he strode into the bedroom.

CHAPTER *Twelve*

"YOU CAN'T MEAN it!" Paula stuffed her robe into the closet and turned to face Tom. "You can't refuse to consider his offer. That's the whole reason for . . . everything!"

"Yes, that's right, it was the whole reason for everything." He pulled his clothes off viciously and flung them across the chair. "I thought I was cured of dashing through life with blinders on, and now I did it again!"

"What?" She wished she could figure out what he was talking about.

"Don't worry about it, Paula," he said shortly. "It's my problem, not yours."

"But what about your . . . plans?"

"I'll find another way." Tom climbed between the covers and lay with his back to her.

Paula sat indecisively on her side of the bed. Was Tom angry at her or at Jacques, or at both of them? He'd been far more lenient than she would have expected, not even blaming her for the mess they were in. But perhaps the shock was beginning to wear off.

She crept into bed and lay there timidly. Tom had never struck her as stubborn, which made it hard to understand why he would turn down a chance to save his company merely because it meant swallowing his pride. Or was that the reason? In a way, he seemed to be angry with himself.

She wished she could shake the nagging suspicion that this was just a gambit to wheedle the best possible terms. Did Tom intend to conveniently change his mind in the morning? It was frustrating trying to put together a jigsaw puzzle with half the pieces missing!

Her thoughts muddled and swirling, Paula fell asleep.

She awoke with a lost feeling, like when she was a little girl and the rain was pouring down outside her window. The very air seemed sad.

We're leaving, she recalled. Going home. This crazy adventure is coming to an end, and it's back to vacuum cleaners and furniture polish for me.

Tom must have arisen earlier; he wasn't in the room and there were no noises from the bathroom. No doubt he was busy making arrangements for their departure.

Did last night really happen? Did Jacques d'Armand really find out that we aren't married, and did I actually tell him he was being insensitive to his wife, and did Tom truly turn down a chance to get the loan? Paula wondered.

Sally wasn't going to believe it. Paula wasn't sure she believed it herself. Well, it had all been part of the great bluff, the poker game with a stake of millions, and Tom had lost. But she'd lost even more.

Half an hour later, after showering and dressing, she emerged. If they were catching a flight out today, she'd better find out what time so she could start packing.

Marie looked up from dusting an end table. "Coffee?"

"Yes, thanks. Have you seen Mr. Clinton?" Paula followed the housekeeper into the kitchen.

"*Oui*. He and Monsieur d'Armand are in conference. If you don't mind, I will wait breakfast until they are finished." Marie poured the coffee into a dainty china cup.

"That's fine." Paula wandered back into the living room and sat down.

Tom and Jacques in conference. There was only one thing they could be talking about... even though Tom had sworn vehemently that he wanted nothing more to do with Jacques.

It's a game, she thought in dismay, resting her chin on the heel of one hand. Strategies planned and revised, every bit of it, and I was just a pawn on the chessboard.

Why did I have to fall in love? she agonized.

She dreaded having to go back to the old routine. Friday mornings were going to be torture. Well, she'd have to get Sally to switch with her. No problem there.

But that wouldn't ease the ache in Paula's heart or the emptiness in her arms when she lay alone at night. She should have known better, after Mickey, than to trust a gambler.

A second cup of coffee joined the first in her stomach as she waited.

Simone, she thought, picturing the elegant blond woman. She'd lost even more than Paula: a husband and a home to which she'd devoted some twenty years of her life. Why did men have to be so unreasonable?

Tom and Jacques didn't show their faces for another hour.

Paula's stomach was snarling a protest by the time the two men entered the living room. They looked as smug as a pair of cats who had just inherited a lifetime supply of cream.

"Good news?" she asked edgily.

Tom nodded. "We've come to an agreement I think we can both live with."

"I'm surprised," Paula admitted. "Last night you were both so adamant."

"It's amazing what a night of reflection can do to one's viewpoint." Jacques led the way onto a terrace, where Marie had set the table for breakfast.

A night of reflection hadn't done much for her own perspective, Paula considered, and this glib pronouncement gave her the strong desire to knock their heads together. But she restrained herself, and sat down at the table instead.

Marie's crêpes were delicious, hunger lending its own spice as the three of them tucked away the thin pancakes filled with fruits and cheeses.

But the repast did nothing to fill the gap in Paula's chest, the sharp disappointment at finding Tom's noble behavior of the previous evening had been a ruse.

Well, there were practical matters to attend to. "Are we leaving today?" she asked Tom when she came up for air.

"I hope that you will be my guests at least until tomorrow," Jacques said.

Tom took a swallow of coffee. "I'd better call the airlines and see what the situation is." He excused himself and went into the house.

Jacques laid aside his napkin and regarded Paula thoughtfully. "Much of this—this happier resolution—is to your credit, you know."

"Mine?" she said, astonished.

He nodded. "What you said about Simone last night—I—well, I never considered that she might doubt my love for her. My father was very strict in the way he ran his household, and my mother approved. It never occurred to me that I was being selfish in expecting Simone to devote herself solely to me."

"I don't remember saying all that," Paula confessed.

Jacques laughed. "Perhaps some of it came from my own thoughts."

"What... what are you going to do?" She was meddling again, Paula realized, but that could hardly make any difference now.

"I telephoned my wife this morning, and we will meet for lunch—privately," Jacques said. "She did not sleep well last night either. Our marriage has been a good one, for a long time, and neither of us can give up on it lightly. We both suffer. And now we will work things out. Together, of course," he added quietly. "How do you Americans say it? In the spirit of compromise?"

Paula crossed her fingers under the table. At least one couple should have a happy ending, she thought. "So you and Tom are on good terms now? I'm glad you're willing to forgive our stupid prank. We must have had air in our brains."

"Tom has explained to me... well... many things," he said enigmatically.

"What about the Jensens?" Paula asked. "Won't they be angry?"

He shrugged. "Perhaps, at first. But they will see the humor, I think, especially when they learn that you really are to be married."

For a moment, Paula couldn't breathe. Really are to be married? How could Tom have told such a bald lie?

She'd fallen for his ruse last night, truly believing that he regretted their escapade. But now he planned to go through the whole farce over again, and he hadn't even bothered to ask her permission!

Somehow she managed to keep her expression composed. It would serve Tom right if she spoiled his plan, but after what they'd been through she decided the price of vengeance might be too high.

All she said was, "I see."

"I am a Frenchman, and I appreciate romance," Jacques continued, regarding her warmly. "There is something touching about it—the two of you making a business arrangement and then falling in love under our noses."

"Yes, it was . . . unexpected." How could Tom be so cruel as to put her in yet another awkward situation? Didn't he care about her feelings, or did he really not suspect how much she cared about him?

"One's emotions have a way of catching one off guard—ah, here he is." Jacques looked up as Tom approached.

"I'm afraid we can't get a flight out until tomorrow anyway, so we're here for the weekend." Tom resumed his seat, apparently noticing nothing amiss. Paula kept her eyes averted.

"Good," said Jacques. "I think tonight we will have even more to celebrate. You will join Simone and me for dinner?"

"As long as it doesn't turn out like last night." Paula managed to pull off the joke, and the two men chuckled appreciatively.

"And if you like—have you visited Monaco?" Jacques asked.

Paula shook her head.

"You can't go home without seeing it, now that you're so close," Jacques said. "Good. Then we are agreed. And perhaps a little sight-seeing first, if Simone wishes."

"We'd like that very much." Tom's eyes glowed with satisfaction. Oh, he was pleased with himself, wasn't he? Paula thought angrily.

She didn't want to say anything in front of Jacques, so she excused herself and went for a walk in the garden.

Marie's crêpes tumbled around in her intestines, undigested, as she reviewed the conversation with Jacques.

Tom had actually had the nerve to say they were getting married! Did he think Jacques wouldn't check? Or that the Jensens would never suspect anything?

This was completely outrageous, beyond anything even Mickey would have attempted. She'd seriously misjudged Tom.

It wasn't worth it, keeping the Clinton Computers account. Even though Sally was going to kill her, Paula couldn't play along any further.

She stalked through the garden, scarcely noticing the scent of roses and the soft summer breeze that ruffled across her hair.

So much had happened here in the short space of four days. Simone's visit . . . the fight over Melina . . . lovemaking in the hot tub . . . and then last night . . .

Tears clouded Paula's vision. Despite her uncertainty, she'd known moments of intense joy at this villa. And pangs of pain greater than anything she'd experienced before. How was she going to keep her composure tonight, watching Simone and Jacques delight in their reconciliation while her own situation was so hopeless?

The sound of the sports car pulling out of the driveway grated on her nerves. It must be almost noon; Jacques had said he was joining his wife for lunch. Tom would probably come looking for her shortly.

Paula wandered unhappily back to their bedroom, entering through the French doors, then stopped and caught her breath.

Tom stood there, naked from the waist up, changing from his button-down shirt into a polo top. The shifting morning light played across his muscular arms and chest, highlighting the gold of his skin.

A tilt of the head acknowledged her presence as Tom hung away his shirt. "I was right about coming to the Riviera."

"What do you mean?" Her jaw ached with the tension of holding back angry words.

"I knew we could persuade him to come up with a more reasonable offer." Tom pulled the polo shirt on over his head. "Thirty-five percent. That's still high for my taste, but it's a lot better than fifty."

"Congratulations," Paula said.

"And he wants the majority on the board of directors, which is understandable." A sigh. "Plus we'll have to go public. A lot of conditions."

"Including a marriage of convenience? Didn't those go out with bustles and hoop skirts, or is it just that we cleaning ladies aren't up on the latest..."

Her words finally got through to him. "Is something bothering you?" A decided understatement!

"Oh, nothing." Paula pulled off the wedding ring

and dropped it in the palm of his hand. "I'm resigning from my position as royal consort. Or should I say concubine?"

"Why do I have the feeling that I came in at the middle of the movie?" he asked, sitting on the edge of the bed and eyeing her quizzically. "Mind filling me in?"

"Oh, Tom, how could you lie to Jacques *again?*" she flared. "To say we were really getting married! That was... that was uncalled for!" She grabbed a brush and tugged it through her hair, fighting against tears.

"I may have mentioned something to that effect, yes," he conceded.

"How did you think we were going to pull that off?" Her voice threatened to crack. "I have no intention of getting involved in any more charades!"

"No one asked you to," Tom said.

"Sally's right: I was completely out of my mind." She tossed the brush on the table and paced across the room. "I should never have let you drag me along to France in the first place. I should never have gone to Malibu—or out to dinner! I should have changed my clothes downstairs in one of the rest rooms and none of this would have happened."

"You're impulsive." He grinned. "What's wrong with that?"

"And now I'm supposed to play at being your wife whenever your partners come to town," she growled. "I suspect that will be rather often."

"It probably will," he said.

"That's great. I'm to be on call at a moment's notice. Maybe I could move some of my clothes into your closets to make it more convincing."

"That's not a bad idea." His eyes twinkled. Blast

him; he was enjoying this!

"No." Paula folded her arms determinedly. "I'm not going to do it. Go ahead and fire me."

"You can't afford to be fired," he pointed out.

"No, but anything would be better than going through this nonsense. Oh, Tom, don't you care about anything but your damn business deals?"

"I'll tell you what." He held out the ring. "First, put this back on."

"I won't." She backed away.

"You look like a child refusing to take castor oil." He chuckled, infuriating her even further. "This is a very expensive ring."

"I'll settle for severance pay."

"Put it back on, and I'll let you keep it." He held out the gleaming ring toward her.

"Tom, that's an insult," she snapped. "You can't buy me off that way. I've already told you, the pretending stops here."

"Maybe we won't have to pretend." Walking over, Tom picked up her hand firmly and slipped the ring into place. "We could get married for real."

Her thoughts flashed back to the first night they'd met, when he said that if he'd known how much help it was, he'd have gotten married long ago. Little had she suspected that he meant it!

"Tom Clinton, I hate you!" She tugged at the ring, but in her fury, her fingers slipped uselessly over the smooth gold. "I'm not some piece of equipment you can buy and sell!"

He looked startled. "That wasn't a business proposition."

"I suppose it was a heartfelt declaration of romantic love?" Pain sharpened her tongue. "Maybe we could have our wedding music composed by a computer, and I'll carry a bouquet of dollar bills! Arthur Jensen could walk me down the aisle."

"Any way you want it," he said. "A big bash at the Century Plaza Hotel, or fifteen minutes in a Las Vegas wedding chapel. Or anything in between. I wasn't feeding Jacques a line, dearest; I really do intend to marry you." He caught her shoulders, forcing her to meet his gaze.

"Don't you think you might have asked me first?" She glared at him, her eyes full of hurt and disappointment. "I'm just another ace in the deck to you, aren't I?"

"Paula, I know the difference between games and real life." He tightened his grasp when she tried to pull away. "You crazy woman, can't you see that I love you?"

To Paula's humiliation, she started to cry. She wanted so much for it to be true. She'd have given anything at that moment to be married to Tom Clinton, to spend the rest of her life with him—but not on the terms he wanted.

No doubt she'd be a great convenience, and he was undoubtedly fond of her. But life together, real life, wasn't the same as romping around the French countryside.

It meant commitment, stability, children. It meant that sometimes he might have to sacrifice what he wanted for what she and the children needed. It meant unselfishness, dependability, trust.

Even if Tom meant it now, she knew too much about gamblers to believe he'd keep up the bargain indefinitely. He'd never be able to sit tight. There was always another game rolling somewhere, another chance to hit it big.

Tom held her close, letting her cry it out. Paula pressed against his soft shirt and felt the firmness of his chest underneath. How she loved him! She could almost bring herself to say yes, do anything to be with him.

Memories of that last year with Mickey flooded back, blotting out the bright Cap-Ferrat sunlight.

It wasn't so much the dingy one-room apartments or the broken-down plumbing or the bill collectors that overwhelmed her. It was Mickey himself. Mickey, always hopeful, always with another plan that was going to make their fortunes. "Just give me one more chance, Paula." "This is it, babe, stick with me." "I met a guy today who has a surefire system..."

Tom was much slicker, of course. There wouldn't be any rundown motels.

But Paula had experienced enough this past week to know that luxurious rooms couldn't hide the dark side of risk taking. The lying, the tricks, the labyrinth of make-believe that cheated you of your self-respect.

Sure, Tom had won this match with Jacques. But he wouldn't be able to stop there. He was too much like Mickey.

"I can't marry you." She stepped away. "I'll wear the ring until we leave France. Then you can make up some reason for a broken engagement. I've had enough, Tom."

"You can't really expect me to give you up." He reached out to touch her hair.

"You don't have a choice." She fumbled for a tissue on the nightstand and blew her nose. It didn't take a mirror to tell her the tears had left her eyes red-rimmed and puffy. That was what came with having a fair complexion.

"Maybe you're the one who doesn't have a choice." Tom's hands played down across her shoulders, massaging the muscles. Paula would have liked to push him away, but tension had cramped her joints and the rubbing felt wonderful.

His fingers probed her shoulder blades. Tom pulled her closer on the pretext of gaining access to more of her back.

"I don't want... I'm not..."

"Relax." Tom drew her down onto the bed. "You're wound up tight. That's no way to enjoy your last day on the Riviera."

She lay on her stomach, letting him explore and banish the stiffness. His touch brought back memories: the weekend in Malibu, the sunlight washing over them on the patio as they massaged each other, the exhilarating smell of hot skin.

His hands moved against the bare flesh of her back, underneath the blouse. The rhythm slowed, became more sensuous as his fingers toyed with the hooks of her bra.

"This is getting in the way." Tom unsnapped it. The nearness of him was raising delicious tingles along her spine.

She loved him in spite of everything. If he'd only forget this insane idea of getting married to impress his associates, maybe it couldn't hurt to be lovers for a while longer... A rationalization, to be sure. She was too involved, had been hurt too badly, to ever treat Tom Clinton casually...

His thumbs circled across her back, to the edge of her breasts. Pressed against the bed, her nipples hardened, and Paula no longer cared what the reason was for her wanting him...

She closed her eyes. There was nothing in the world but the whisper of his breathing and the tantalizing pressure on her sides, ribs, breasts.

Strong hands slid underneath her chest, catching the mounds and kneading them. Paula moaned softly and raised herself on her elbows to give him more freedom.

And he took it, caressing down along her stomach toward the waistband of her jeans.

"Marry me, Paula," he whispered.

"No." She had to force the word out.

He pressed down over her, chest against her back, hips tight to her derriere, his masculine hardness unmistakable. She wanted him to be part of her. Now.

"Tom." Paula rolled over, catching him around the neck and pulling him into a kiss. His tongue tasted her swollen lips, flicked across her teeth, and hesitated at the entrance to her mouth.

She took the initiative, meeting his tongue with her own, luring him inside her and making him welcome there. As the kiss deepened, his hands stimulated her breasts until she thought she would go mad with desire.

Slowly he unfastened her jeans. Then he lifted his head. "Marry me."

"Make love to me," she answered.

"Marriage or nothing." To her dismay, he swung off her. "We'd better get ready for our tour. Jacques and Simone could be back any time."

"You rat!"

A gleam of teeth. The rascal was laughing at her!

Paula picked up her pillow and swung it full force. It thumped against Tom's arm. "I'll teach you to be a tease!"

"What?" He backed away, feigning innocence. "You think I would let my pure, virginal body be used for nonmarital lust?"

"Pure, virginal body, hogwash!" Paula jumped up to pursue him, trying to ignore his friendly leer at her bare breasts. "You're trying to blackmail me!"

"Not blackmail," he protested. "Just to catch you in a vulnerable moment."

Whack! went the pillow. "You think you can manipulate anybody, don't you?" She was half angry and half amused, and terribly hungry for him.

"Hey! Is that any way to treat your boss?" He skirted a chair in his efforts to escape.

"The only way!" To her dismay, she saw that he was heading for the door. "You can't get off that easily!"

"You're going to follow me out?" His eyes swept down her nude front, and Paula realized her nipples were still taut with longing. "You'd certainly make a sight Marie wouldn't forget soon. Or Jacques. I think I heard a car in the driveway..."

"Well, great!" She whumped him again with the pillow, for good measure. "Isn't that the idea? Maybe it'll impress him so much he'll come down to twenty-five percent!"

Tom leaned against the wall and chuckled. Paula couldn't help it; she joined in.

"All right," she said. "I'm letting you off the hook...this time. But tonight, buster, you'd better deliver the goods."

"Only if you promise to marry me." He dodged out of the room and closed the door.

Paula changed into slacks. Oh, how she loved that man. But she couldn't, wouldn't let herself give in.

CHAPTER
Thirteen

IT WAS SEVERAL hours before Jacques and Simone appeared, and when they did their flushed faces and broad smiles made Paula suspect that their reunion had not been a platonic one.

The blond woman caught Paula's hands and drew her aside. "I'm so happy for both of us," she said. "It was a shock to learn you and Tom were not married, but to know that you fell in love under our roof—well, that more than makes up for it!"

The last thing Paula wanted was to mar her friend's joy, so she merely nodded. "Jacques is going to let you work with the theater company?"

"Oh, yes," Simone said. "We will live here together until the play is done. It's only a few months. Sometimes he will have to go to Paris, but mostly he will take a little—a big— vacation." She smiled. "And then perhaps we can come to see you in California!"

"We'd love that," Paula said, regretting the disappointment her friend would feel later, when she learned of the "broken engagment."

Jacques had gone into the house with his wife's

suitcases, and Simone added in a low voice, "Thank you for speaking up for me. Apparently what you said made a big difference."

"Tom had a good bit to say to Jacques, too," Paula admitted, not wanting to take undue credit. "I'm afraid we called your husband a few unflattering names—like insensitive and stiff-necked, or something to that effect."

"And he deserved it." Simone laughed. "But I love him anyway. He has many good qualities, and now that I have my own work for part of the year, I know our life together will be far better than before."

The men joined them, and they set out for their sight-seeing. Paula had expected a brief tour, but Jacques and Simone overflowed with enthusiasm and wanted to show their guests everything.

Paula had always thought of the Côte d'Azur as a playground for the rich, but that afternoon she discovered that it was also a treasure house of art and relics.

They visited museums devoted to Chagall, Matisse, and Picasso, and returned to St-Paul-de-Vence, where memories of their dinner flooded back. However, Paula quickly brushed them aside in her wonder at the Maeght Foundation, where the architecture blended an intriguing collection of modern artworks into the landscaping.

From time to time, Tom would touch Paula in subtle ways—a hand on her shoulder, his arm slipped through hers, a mild collision once when they turned toward each other unexpectedly.

The recurrent contact and the musky scent of him kept desire simmering just below the surface. Fortunately, their hosts were too wrapped up in their own feelings to notice.

"Perhaps we'd better go home to change before dinner," Jacques suggested at last, his arm circling Simone's waist. "And then we will have our visit to Monaco."

"Wonderful," Paula agreed.

The four of them retreated to the villa, where Jacques and Simone hurried off to their own end of the house, apparently eager to renew their celebration.

Feeling a bit envious, Paula followed Tom to their bedroom.

"You owe me something," she told him as she removed her clothing. He stood by the closet, unbuttoning his shirt.

"I think I walked too much." He feigned a huge yawn. "Exercise always makes me sleepy. Think I have time for a nap?"

"You fake!" She was torn between amusement and frustration.

"You have only to say the word and my body is yours." Tom pulled off his shirt and bared his well-shaped chest. Paula longed to run her fingers across the hair that curled down to a V. "Just promise to marry me."

"You can't hold out forever!" She stretched atop the covers invitingly.

"Neither can you, I hope." His trousers came off, Paula closed her eyes against the sight of his lean, inviting body.

He couldn't seriously believe she'd let herself be seduced into marrying him! Yet wasn't that just like Tom, to turn this into a contest of wills? He was betting that she'd say yes, but she'd finally learned that gambling didn't pay.

The mattress sank a little as he lay down beside her. A leg brushed against hers, accidentally on purpose. Paula leaned over and bit his arm.

"Ouch!" Tom clasped his arm dramatically. "No need to turn vicious!"

"That's what happens when I'm thwarted." She pretended to bite him again.

"I'll tame you, my little wolverine." Tom pinned her shoulders down against the bed. "There! Bite away, and you'll get only air for your pains."

"That's what you think." She glanced meaningfully at his body, poised over hers. "Now I've got you where I want you."

"Say it," he urged. "'Yes, I'll marry you.'"

"Yes, I'll sleep with you," she said.

"I'll make an honest woman of you yet," he announced, letting go and flopping onto his side of the bed. "Or you'll die of terminal passion."

"Not before you do." Paula turned over, giving up for the moment. What an infuriating man he was!

They dozed for about an hour, until they heard noises indicating their hosts were back in circulation. Paula awoke slowly, and by the time she got up Tom had already gone out.

As she pulled on her new pink dress, Paula looked around her wistfully. She knew it was an illusion, but she couldn't help feeling that as long as she and Tom remained here, they were safe.

Well, she'd better prepare herself, because reality in the form of Sally and a vacuum cleaner were only forty-eight hours away.

Paula trailed into the bathroom to brush her hair. She was definitely going to have to get it cut, by someone other than Sally. Well, she would be able to afford it when Tom paid her...

I don't want Tom to pay me! she thought fiercely.

I want him to keep me with him!

She set the brush down on the sink and gazed at herself in the mirror, for the first time letting herself seriously consider his offer.

How tempting it was: Marriage to the man she loved. Travel, exquisite surroundings, dinner at the best restaurants, riding about in one of his expensive cars. Everything money could buy.

But that wasn't what she wanted. No, she corrected herself, she certainly wouldn't turn up her nose at luxury, but it wasn't enough. The things she needed most, Tom wasn't offering.

She fastened on a pair of turquoise earrings. Tonight she was going to enjoy herself. Unless . . .

A thread of fear tightened in her stomach. They'd be going to the casino. Surely Tom wouldn't be foolish enough to gamble too heavily, not in front of Jacques. But maybe he couldn't help it.

This sinking feeling took her back to the days with Mickey, that constant undercurrent of dread. No, she refused to live this way for the rest of her life.

There was nothing she could do about it tonight, she reminded herself forcefully, and went out to join the others.

Simone looked stunning in a gown of silver-blue, and happiness had softened the harsh planes of Jacques's face so that he was handsome indeed. What an attractive couple they made, Paula thought as they drove along the coast to Monaco.

The d'Armands selected a restaurant on the cliffs of Monte Carlo, overlooking the Mediterranean. The sea sparkled with reflected light, and Paula gazed across the water, trying to imagine the sailors who had passed this way over the ages, from the ancient

Egyptians to modern Greek tycoons.

They dined on fresh seafood, and Paula allowed herself a *mousse au chocolat* for dessert. Simone chattered merrily about the role she was to play in the theatrical production, and Jacques looked proud of her.

Yet throughout the meal, Paula was conscious of a sense of unease. She wished they could go directly back to the villa, but she knew Jacques looked forward to showing them the city's most famous sight.

If only he were like the Jensens, who, Paula recalled, didn't even bet money at cards. But naturally a European saw no vice in gambling.

Finally the last glass of wine had been drunk and the last wisp of dessert savored. Doing her best to hide her reluctance, Paula rose with the others.

The casino of Monte Carlo, set amid formal gardens, displayed an ornate grandeur that reminded her of the opera house in Paris. Paula kept silent as they walked toward the entrance, only half listening to the historical data with which Jacques regaled them.

The interior surpassed anything in Vegas. Red velvet curtains, crystal chandeliers, an atmosphere of elegant restraint—the clicks and calls and murmurs were hushed, not raised to a deafening roar as in the casinos back home.

"Do you care for baccarat?" Jacques asked. "That was the favorite of the fictional spy James Bond."

It was also a game played for very high stakes. Paula held her breath.

"No, thanks," Tom said cheerfully. "Roulette is more my style."

"The odds are terrible," she couldn't resist pointing out. Mickey had preferred craps, but she wasn't even sure if they played that here.

"In America, yes," Tom said. "The Europeans play roulette differently. The odds still favor the house, of course, but not by such an outrageous margin."

Jacques led the way to the roulette table, where three well-dressed men and two older women were laying their bets.

"The French people would not stand for the American system, which is most unfair. Roulette is a game they take very seriously," Simone added, her hand resting on her husband's arm as they watched the muted play on the green baize table.

Paula studied the game board and the roulette wheel. "Looks the same to me."

"Observe more closely." Tom waited.

"Oh. There's no slot for double zero," she said.

"Therefore one fewer space on the table, and one fewer chance to lose."

"There is also a difference in the rules, but I doubt you are interested in a lesson in gambling," Jacques noted as Tom bought a stack of chips.

That was true. She'd had enough lessons in gambling to last a lifetime.

Paula glanced at Tom's chips. "They're all the same color." She indicated the chips held by other players. "How can you tell whose are whose?"

"You have to pay attention." He began to place his bets.

Paula watched for several spins of the wheel, as the stack of chips dwindled. "What's your system?"

"When I win, I double up. When I lose, I don't," he said.

It took Paula a minute to figure that one out. Mickey had doubled his bets at every play, believing that when he did win, he'd win big. "Does it work?"

"About forty-nine percent of the time," Tom conceded. "The other fifty-one percent, the house wins. Which beats fifty-five percent back in the States."

He was betting on zero and the numbers two, four, and twenty-four. She remembered that the Clinton Computers Building street number was 2440.

On the fourth time out, Tom began to win.

"I may break even on this," he joked.

Jacques smiled. "I always arrange a winning streak for my guests. You will see."

Tom won again on the fifth round, but lost on the sixth. He won again on the seventh.

There was a kind of fascination in watching the little ball spin around and suddenly, arbitrarily, drop into a slot. Even Paula felt the hypnotic effect.

And seeing Tom win made victory look easy. As it always did, no matter who was winning. She knew this feeling from her own instincts as well as Mickey's. If she bet on her license plate number or her phone number or her address, she'd be sure to make a bundle.

Tom won the eighth round.

People were beginning to gather, muttering to each other. Some of them added bets to Tom's, so that he had to keep close tabs on which chips belonged to him.

The ninth round he lost. And the tenth. The stack in front of Tom began to shorten again.

The other players went back to their own systems. Some of the onlookers drifted away.

Tom won the eleventh round. Lost the twelfth. Won the thirteenth. And from there he won three in a row.

A pit boss, or whatever they were called in France, came over and examined the wheel. A soft-spoken conference with the croupiers, and the play continued.

Another loss, and then two wins. The fickle onlookers drifted back. More bets were placed on the board. Some people were clearly betting against Tom, expecting his luck to change.

And it did.

He began to lose. As he'd said, he didn't increase his bets, but they'd reached such large proportions by now that his chips vanished at an alarming rate.

Tom watched the wheel with narrow eyes, a muscle twitching in his cheek. Completely absorbed. Paula doubted whether he would have noiced if she and the d'Armands left. She'd seen Mickey stand at the craps table cursing the croupiers when they fled during a fire at a Vegas hotel. Two firemen had to drag him out.

Tom won again, but it was only a quirk. He lost the next round, and the one after that.

Paula knew what was going to happen as she watched the last of the chips go onto the board. He would buy more. And more. As long as his cash held out, and maybe his credit.

She glanced at Jacques. His expression was bland, unreadable. But she knew he was paying close attention. Simone looked slightly alarmed.

The wheel spun. One of the croupiers scraped up the last of the chips.

"You win some, you lose some." Tom grinned. And stepped away from the table.

"I will make good your loss, of course," Jacques said.

"Nonsense." Tom held up his hand for emphasis.

"I'm a big boy. I knew what I was doing. Besides, I didn't lose much. If I'd blown the plane fare home, I might accept."

"I thought..." Paula let the words trail away as they crossed the casino, pausing to observe the various games in progress. They even had slot machines here, she noted with wry amusement.

"Gambling—it is a kind of adventure, no?" Jacques said as they emerged into the warm clear night.

"A kind of cheap thrills," Tom corrected. "There's a certain challenge to it, especially when there's a skill involved. But it takes more foolhardiness than courage."

"Didn't you think your luck would turn?" Paula knew exactly how Mickey's line of reasoning would run. "After all, you'd been on a winning streak. Maybe that was just a short break."

"Maybe." Tom helped her into the car. "And maybe it was just the start of a long downhill slide."

In the silence of the car, Paula realized that her heart was thumping wildly. She'd been more afraid than she had suspected.

Tom slid in beside her. Her body vibrated with the pressure of his hip against hers, the brightness in his eyes, the quickness of his breathing tickling against her neck.

Gambling was exciting, no matter what he said. His adrenaline was pumping. And so was hers.

Simone smiled back at them gaily as Jacques started the engine and pulled out of the parking space. So she felt relieved also.

"I hate to leave France," Paula said.

"But you will come back," Simone assured her as

they navigated the hilly streets of Monte Carlo. "Tom and Jacques will be partners. After you're married, we will see each other often."

I wouldn't count on it, she thought, but managed to refrain from speaking.

"We hope to be able to return your hospitality," Tom assured her. "We'd love to have you stay with us for as long as you like."

Stay with them? The man was acting as if this marriage would actually take place! Hadn't he believed her? Or was he just playing out the game until the last hand was dealt?

Paula's thoughts eddied as the car raced through the Mediterranean night, west to Cap-Ferrat.

Tom's behavior at the roulette table had surprised her. Was that what he intended? Had the entire demonstration been staged for her benefit?

Even so, whatever the "stakes," Mickey would not have been able to stop. Just as he hadn't been able to call a halt when gambling ruined his work, dissipated his savings, and destroyed his marriage. Nothing meant more than the possibility that the next roll of the dice might change his luck.

Had she been wrong about Tom? she wondered, regarding his profile, black against the deep gray of the night. But why had securing the loan meant so much to him? His compulsive gambling might be limited to the boardroom—as Tom had said, he played for higher stakes—but did that make it any less a problem?

A movement, and his hand touched her neck beneath the shaggy hair. A gentle, kneading motion; she closed her eyes. Neither of them looked at the other as her senses focused on that tender stroking.

Paula could hardly breathe.

It was so close, everything she wanted out of life. So close that it couldn't possibly be real.

She remembered another drive through the night, in her childhood. To a Fourth of July fireworks celebration.

For days she'd looked forward to it. Paula loved to read fairy tales, and from her parents' descriptions she was sure this would be a magical experience.

She'd grown up on Army bases, moving from one to another every few years, leaving friends behind, finally hesitating to make new ones. The towns where they stayed were small and bleakly unwelcoming to an imaginative, shy little girl.

The brilliant Fourth of July display was going to make up for it. En route, she had leaned forward in the car, childishly trying to make the vehicle move faster.

Then they arrived, and the fireworks started. Blazes of scarlet, yellow, and blue streamed across the night sky. Umbrellas of color opened before her eyes. Just as her parents had said.

But it didn't make up for anything. No angel came down from the heavens and granted all her wishes. No fairy godmother appeared to turn her T-shirt and shorts into a splendid ballgown, her pumpkin into a coach. Fireworks were only colored lights in the sky . . .

What about Tom? She envisioned so many things, such happiness within their grasp. Nights of lying side by side, laughter, a baby waving perfect tiny hands as it cuddled in her arms.

Was this merely an illusion, too?

Tom seemed to sense her distress. He slipped his arm around her and pulled her closer. The warmth of his body felt good against her cool skin.

They rode home in silence.

CHAPTER
Fourteen

"WHAT'S GOING THROUGH that head of yours?" Tom said as he closed the bedroom door behind them.

"I don't know." Paula sank into a chair. "Maybe I'm just depressed about leaving France. I've had such a wonderful time here."

"We could come back on our honeymoon," he suggested.

"Bribery?" She gave him a weak smile.

"Paula, I know your ex-husband was a gambler." He sat on the foot of the bed, facing her. "So am I, but in a different way. I thought I showed you that. I only gamble deep when the odds are better than fifty-fifty. And I know when to quit."

She tried to formulate her thoughts into words. "Marriage isn't a business deal, Tom. It isn't something you take a chance on and hope to win. It's little things, every day. Sometimes it can get boring."

"Do you honestly believe my attention span is limited to a few days, or weeks?" His tan eyes bored into hers. "That I have no stomach for toughing out hard times? I'm not What's-his-name. I'm me, Tom. How about giving me a chance?"

A lump stuck in her throat, and Paula had trouble pushing the words out. "I have given you a chance. A lot of them. But you don't even trust me enough to tell me what's on your mind."

"What haven't I told you? I've told you everything that involves you." His voice sounded strained.

"Everything that involves me?" Paula's temper flared. "You don't even trust me to keep my mouth shut if you've got some other investment deal going! You said you had 'reasons.' Reasons for why the loan from Jacques meant so much. What else do you have going, Tom? Or is it something so dishonest you're ashamed of it?"

Tom stared at her in amazement. "You think I'm up to something... something underhanded?"

"What else am I supposed to think?" Tears trembled on the edge of her vision. "You've done nothing since I met you but worry about making money, even when you had to lie to do it."

He reached out and caught her hands. "In a way you're right, Paula. I'm self-centered, and I'm probably also simpleminded, but... it isn't what you think."

"If you were serious about wanting to marry me, you wouldn't be keeping me in the dark." Paula bit her lip, hard, to stop the threatened flood.

"All right. It goes back to when I first made money." He stared down at the floor, looking ashamed and angry at the same time. "I wallowed in it. After years of struggling, finally I could travel, buy fine clothes—everything I wanted. And I did."

"Nobody could blame you for that," Paula said.

"I could." The words emerged, harsh with recrimination. "Just about the time the crunch came along,

I ran across a news article concerning a summer camp for kids with cancer. It was about to fold because it lacked funds."

"Your sister died of cancer, didn't she?" Paula thought of the photograph and the girl in the wheelchair.

"Yes. And you know the one thing she always wanted? To ride a horse. That's all, just to ride a horse. She never got to do it. Well, that's what this camp is for: to let kids like her have a little joy in their short lives." He shook his head, as if breaking through painful memories.

"So you wanted to raise money for the camp?" she said.

"I want to do more than that. I want to set up a foundation that will ensure the camp never lacks for funds again. And I discovered there are organizations that grant dying children their last wishes," Tom went on. "I want to help them, too."

"Why didn't you tell me?" Paula wished she could wipe away the hurt on his face.

"Oh, sure, I could've made myself out to be a real hero. Just to impress you—and the d'Armands, too, and everybody else." He clasped her hands tightly within his large, warm ones. "Paula, I don't deserve that kind of credit. And I'm not saying that I didn't want to save Clinton Computers, too. My own skin, as it were. If I were strictly honest, I'd have to say that the two goals are equally important—bailing out my company and setting up the fund to run the camp. Besides, Paula, the camp... well... it's something I owe my sister, that's all. It's.... private."

Paula had listened quietly, letting all this register. "But why did you tell Jacques you wouldn't discuss a second offer then?" she said at last.

"It wasn't till last night that I saw how insensitive I'd been—pursuing my 'noble quest' without a thought for anyone else," he said. "I had no right to force you to pretend to be my wife. No right to dupe Jacques. I decided it was time to call a halt."

"What changed your mind?" This was a new side of Tom, this introspective man who held himself up to incredibly high standards, and Paula felt suddenly shy with him.

"You. Curled up there beside me, so trusting and vulnerable." His lips brushed hers. "Like those kids. I decided to do it for them, and maybe to make up to you for what I'd put you through."

"You should have told me," she whispered, remembering her unfounded suspicion that he'd been manipulating her and Jacques all over again. "You can't take the whole world on your shoulders, Tom."

He pulled her out of the chair and onto the bed beside him. "I love you, Paula." His lips brushed her forehead, touched her moist eyelids, traced her nose, and found her mouth. "I guess I'm not an easy man to live with. But please say you'll try."

"I love you, too," she said, and forgot about speaking in the surrender of a kiss.

This was different—this lovemaking—from anything they'd shared before. Instead of hot urgency, she felt a delicious ache softened by the certainty that Tom would cure it.

His breath warmed her neck, the hollow of her collarbone, the swell of cleavage.

When he unzipped her dress, she helped him pull it off, wanting nothing to keep them apart. She lifted away her slip and was about to unsnap her bra when he stopped her.

"Let me do it." Tom turned her so that her back

was to him, and his fingers danced enticingly along the line of the bra before loosening it.

From behind, his arms encircled her and his hands cupped her breasts. Moist kisses played across her shoulders, and Paula gave herself over to the tingling sensations radiating from the firm nipples to the rest of her body.

Tom explored lower, removing the lacy wisp of panties, stroking her soft core, drawing forth a moan of ecstasy.

"Wait." Paula lay against him for a breathless moment. "I want to share this with you."

She swung around to face him, melting beneath the tenderness in his eyes. Fumblingly, she removed his clothes.

He sat bare to her gaze, his body glowing and perfect in the lamplight.

"Lie down," she said. With a quirk of the eyebrow, he obeyed.

It was her turn to sample Tom, to nibble at the fine brown hair, to knead away the tension from his neck and shoulders, to run her fingers through the curly mat on his chest.

She followed the line of hair to his flat belly, smoothing her hands along the muscular thighs and then to his hardness, cradling, rubbing, arousing in him the overwhelming hunger he had created in her.

Every nerve ending in her was attuned to him, sensitive as a fine antenna. She noted every quiver of response, every intake of breath.

Then her own needs demanded satisfaction. Paula stretched out alongside Tom, feeling the skin of their legs brush, her hips wedge against his, the erect points of her breasts press into his chest.

"Say it, Paula." He was hoarse with passion.

"What?" For a minute she couldn't make sense of his demand, and then she remembered. How like Tom, to think of a thing like that at a time like this! "Yes, I'll marry you, Thomas C. Clinton the Third."

"I thought you'd never say it." He rolled on top of her, and with barely restrained roughness, his mouth tantalized her yielding breasts into swollen readiness.

Fierce heat coursed through her deepest self, ready for him. And then he was there, one with her, coiled tension releasing itself with drive after drive that only increased her longing.

Paula clawed him in her eagerness, twisting against him. She urged him on with her mouth and breasts and legs.

The explosion was like nothing she had ever experienced before. Her body fused with his, quaked, and sent nerves rioting into a new dimension of light and color.

Paula hovered in the center of brilliance, wondering at the wave after wave of fulfillment that splashed across her.

It was more than physical, this ecstasy she felt. This was coming home, feeling safe and loved, looking forward to a life of joy and spontaneity and security.

"Oh, Tom." She lay against him in a tangle of damp flesh and happiness.

Fireworks. Oddly, she recalled again that disappointing night of her childhood. How pale the pyrotechnics had seemed beside her imaginings.

But not tonight. She could never have anticipated anything like this. It was more. More than having one's wishes come true, more than being drawn into a magic world. It was all those things, but it was also love.

"Not having second thoughts, are you?" he teased, lifting himself on one elbow. "I'll tell you what."

"What?" Paula couldn't resist stroking a rebellious wisp of hair that stood up from his head.

"If you marry me, I promise you'll never have to clean anything again," Tom said.

Her eyes flew wide in mock astonishment. "Why didn't you say that in the first place? I'd have married you in a minute!"

"Then all that's left is to get a blood test and set the date." He flopped back on the bed, looking quite pleased with himself. Paula began to laugh. "What?" he demanded.

"Sally. My roommate." Paula shook her head. "Can you imagine her reaction?"

"She did strike me as a bit on the skeptical side when we spoke on the phone," he agreed.

"Sally as maid of honor." Paula tried to picture her friend smiling demurely and carrying a bouquet of flowers, but she kept seeing Sally's face with her mouth wide open and her eyes blinking in perpetual surprise. "We'd better have her sign the marriage license or she'll never believe it's for real."

"Just as long as she doesn't come on the honeymoon." Tom stroked one hand along the velvet skin of Paula's back.

Honeymoon. Paula closed her eyes. Tropical beaches and soft summer nights. Or Paris or . . . With a quiver of delight, she realized they could go anywhere in the world. "Hawaii?" she suggested.

"Huh?"

"For our honeymoon, dope." She brushed the rebellious wisp of hair down again, and it sprang right back.

Tom frowned. "I hadn't thought about that. Not in tangible terms, anyway. We've got to get the expansion underway as quickly as possible. I probably won't be able to take more than a few days, at least not for a while."

Paula bit her lip to hold back the disappointment. "Well, I suppose there are plenty of places to go for a weekend near Southern California."

"Malibu?" he teased.

"Tom Clinton!" She glared at him. "You're not planning to conduct business on our honeymoon!"

"Don't worry." His hand cupped hers. "I'm not that big a fool." He pondered for a moment. "We could go to the desert."

"Death Valley in August?" Paula shook her head in disbelief. "Hey, if you want me to melt, just murmur sweet nothings in my ear."

He leaned over and whispered, "Nothing, nothing, nothing. Las Vegas."

"What?"

"Vegas."

"What's that got to do with sweet nothings?"

"It's in the desert," he explained, adding, "We could take in some shows, eat at those magnificent buffets—the more I think about it, the more I like the idea."

Paula shifted uncomfortably on the bed. She'd spent painful hours in that gambling mecca. "Tom, I hate to be a spoilsport, but for me, Vegas doesn't have the world's most wonderful associations."

His expression sobered. "I didn't think about that. You went there with your ex-husband?"

"Often." She could already hear the *ching-ching* of the slot machines.

"Paula, we can go somewhere else." But he looked disappointed.

Then, in a flash, she knew it didn't matter. "No. Let's do it, Tom."

"You sure? There's always Palm springs. Or Santa Barbara."

Paula began to smile. "Remember how scared I was at Monte Carlo? It isn't the casino, it isn't the gaming tables, and it isn't the lure of winning that's dangerous. It's the gambler himself."

"Oh?" His thumb brushed her cheek lovingly. "And I've passed the test?"

"With flying colors," she agreed.

Tom grinned. "Then I'm in? No more hurdles to jump, mountains to climb, or fair maidens to rescue from rampaging vacuum cleaners?"

"Well, there is one other thing," Paula murmured.

"Oh?"

"If you ever ask me to participate in another masquerade like this, I'll divorce you."

"Don't worry." Tom laughed. "From now on I'm going to be a pillar of the community. Book-of-the-Month Club. Subscription to *Reader's Digest*. My only amusement will be building ships out of toothpicks and assembling them inside whiskey bottles."

"That sounds boring," she said.

"Oh, I'll be boring." He leaned over and kissed the tip of her nose. "I solemnly do swear that I will never in my life do anything again that will cause you shame, embarrassment, discomfort, or a twinge of worry."

Then he winked knowingly. "But don't bet on it."

QUESTIONNAIRE

1. How do you rate ______________________________
(please print TITLE)
☐ excellent ☐ good
☐ very good ☐ fair ☐ poor

2. How likely are you to purchase another book in this series?
☐ definitely would purchase
☐ probably would purchase
☐ probably would not purchase
☐ definitely would not purchase

3. How likely are you to purchase another book by this author?
☐ definitely would purchase
☐ probably would purchase
☐ probably would not purchase
☐ definitely would not purchase

4. How does this book compare to books in other contemporary romance lines?
☐ much better
☐ better
☐ about the same
☐ not as good
☐ definitely not as good

5. Why did you buy this book? (Check as many as apply)
☐ I have read other SECOND CHANCE AT LOVE romances
☐ friend's recommendation
☐ bookseller's recommendation
☐ art on the front cover
☐ description of the plot on the back cover
☐ book review I read
☐ other ______________________________
____
____

(Continued...)

6. Please list your three favorite contemporary romance lines.

____

____

7. Please list your favorite authors of contemporary romance lines.

____

____

____

____

____

____

8. How many SECOND CHANCE AT LOVE romances have you read? __________

9. How many series romances like SECOND CHANCE AT LOVE do you <u>read</u> each month? __________

10. How many series romances like SECOND CHANCE AT LOVE do you <u>buy</u> each month? __________

11. Mind telling your age?

☐ under 18
☐ 18 to 30
☐ 31 to 45
☐ over 45

☐ Please check if you'd like to receive our <u>free</u> SECOND CHANCE AT LOVE Newsletter.

We hope you'll share your other ideas about romances with us on an additional sheet and attach it securely to this questionnaire.

• •

Fill in your name and address below:

Name ____________________

Street Address ____________________

City __________ State __________ Zip __________

Please return this questionnaire to:

SECOND CHANCE AT LOVE
The Berkley Publishing Group
200 Madison Avenue, New York, New York 10016